ROMAN JEWELS
A Play

ROMAN JEWELS
A Play

Chapel Orahamm

Portions of this book were previously published under the title "Roman Jewels" in the anthology *In the Wake of the Kraken* (2022, Skullgate Media)

ISBN 978-1-956042-09-2

Ebook ISBN 978-1-956042-10-8

www.skullgatemedia.com

First edition

All images were designed and licensed through Canva

Internal layout by Chris Vandyke

ALSO FROM SKULLGATE MEDIA

TALES FROM THE YEAR BETWEEN

Volume 1—Achten Tan: Land of Dust & Bone

Volume 2—Under New Suns

Volume 3—In The Wake of the Kraken

Volume 4—New Albion (Books 1-4 coming Fall 2022)

SKULLGATE MEDIA PRESENTS

Loathsome Voyages: An Anthology of Weird-Fiction

Winter Wonders

THE LYTHINALL SERIES, by Michael D. Nadeau

The Darkness Returns

The Darkness Within

*The Darkness Rises (*coming soon!*)*

Tales From Lythinall

OTHER BOOKS

Friends of the Skullgate, curated by C. Van Dyke

Each Little Universe, by Chris Durston

Speechless, by Debbie Iancu-Haddad

Roman Jewels: A Play, by Chapel Orahamm

For my Family

A book must be the axe for the frozen sea within us.

— FRANZ KAFKA

Table of Contents

CAST

DRAMATIS PERSONAE

Governor: Overseer of Squanderer's Bay.
Malone: Friend and shipmate of Roman Verne on *The Crimson Blade*. Distant relation to Governor.
Captain Parker: Captain in His Majesty's navy.
Gunner: Servant of Captain Parker.
Lieutenant: Lieutenant under Captain Parker's command.
Ensign: Seaman serving under Captain Parker.
Midshipman: Seaman serving under Captain Parker.
Sailor: Seaman serving under Captain Parker.

Captain Montgomery: Captain of *The Crimson Blade*.
Sailing Master Monsell: Sailing master of *The Crimson Blade*.
Roman Verne: Quartermaster of *The Crimson Blade*.
Bostock: Crew of *The Crimson Blade*. Friend of Roman Verne.
Annesley: Crew of *The Crimson Blade*
Babe: Roman Verne's servant.

Captain Lutterell: Captain of *The Black Albatross*.
Sailing Master Luther: Sailing master of *The Black Albatross*.
Jules Road: Quartermaster of *The Black Albatross*.

Tyndall: Crew of *The Black Albatross*. Swordfighter.
Boatswain: Elderly companion of Captain Lutterell.
Doc: Ship's doctor to *The Black Albatross*.
Palmer: Cabin boy to *The Black Albatross*.
Sanderson: Crew of *The Black Albatross*.
Godfrey: Crew of *The Black Albatross*.
Galley Help: Helps the Cook on *The Black Albatross*.
First Galley Help: Helps the Cook on *The Black Albatross*.
Second Galley Help: Helps the Cook on *The Black Albatross*.
Jefferson: Seaman on *The Black Albatross*.

Madam Linley: Captain of *The Red Lantern*. Brothel madam.
Madam Josephine: Brothel madam with residence on *The Red Lantern*.
Jeweller: Businessman in Half-Moon Bay
Market Watch
Community Leaders
Chorus

ACT 1

PROLOGUE

PROLOGUE
Act 1

Enter Chorus

Chorus:
Two ships' crews, both alike in disposition,
In shadowed Squand'rer's Bay, where th' tale unfolds,
From old insults arise a perturbed mission,
Where privateer treasure lays in blood-bound holds.
From Pirate Code ink of these two captains
A duo of course-crossed lovers escape their fate;
Whose curious discoveries and happ'nings
Do with their stealth steal their captains' estate.
The tempestuous voyage of their cutlass-scarred love,
And the persistence of their captains' deck
Which, save quartermasters' mutiny, none would move,
Is the few hours' rambling on our wreck;
Those of you who wish a moment's entertainment
We shall reach for your desired attainment.

Exeunt all

SCENE 1

ACT 1, SCENE 1

SQUANDERER'S BAY: THE MARKET CENTRE

Enter Sanderson and Godfrey, the crew of Captain Lutterell's The Black Albatross, armed

Sanderson: Godfrey, I promise you, they won't make us into clowns.

Godfrey: Well, duh, we'd be a clown posse and not privateer, and I'm contracted to the code.

Sanderson: Not what I meant, God. I meant, if they cross us, we'd snuff 'em.

Godfrey: Sandy, you might want to see a priest or an apothecary.

Sanderson: Someone pushes my buttons, I push back.

Godfrey: But you don't wear buttons, at least none I've seen.

Sanderson: One of those Montgomery cutthroats pushes my buttons.

Godfrey: I mean, there are some fine-looking specimens on board. Button pushing doesn't sound half bad, does it?

Sanderson: They'd steal my buttons and leave me hanging. Rather crowd the market stalls then share the throughway with one of Montgomery's lackeys.

Godfrey: That's rather nice, giving them some room to get by.

Sanderson: I'm not nice. Women are nice. Here's what I'll do. Montgomery's men can stick to the street, and I'll stick to her women.

Godfrey: Always fighting between The Black Albatross and The Crimson Blade captains. We just work for them.

Sanderson: When I'm captain, I'll put the men in their place and play sweet with the women—I hear they like bananas.

Godfrey: Are we really doing the 'banana in my pocket' joke?

Sanderson: Well, I was till you ruined it.

Godfrey: The joke'd work if you had anything resembling a banana.

Sanderson: I've seen enough bananas around here to know mine's a decent size.

Godfrey: Oh, aye. There's those Lady Fingers that'd give you a run for your money. Oye, here comes trouble. Get out your knife and not your Lady Finger, mind you, lest you think that'll make the Montgomery men skat.

Sanderson: It's out. You initiate. I'll protect your back.

Godfrey: And you'll say you were there in my blind spot the whole time while cowering behind a barrel.

Sanderson: Don't be scared for me.

Godfrey: Yo. You scare me.

Sanderson: Wait. Gov'll have us if we go
pointing bananas, I mean swords, at people.
Let the Montgomerys come over here.

Godfrey: Y'all tell me I have resting bitch face. Of
course, they'll come over. They always do if
I'm around.

Sanderson: I can always flip 'em off. Keep it
subtle, though. They'll have to come over if
your pretty face doesn't do it. (Sanderson
scratches his face with his middle finger,
which just so happens to double as flipping
them off.)

Enter Annesley

Annesley: Shark bait, you flipping us off?

Sanderson: You've gotta be blind if you're
asking.

Annesley: Seriously? Are you a kid or just
looking for a smackdown?

Sanderson: (whispered to Godfrey) Can I call
this self-defence if I say yes and he
attacks me?

Godfrey: (whispered to Sanderson) Nope.

Sanderson: (to Annesley) Uh. No. Not flipping
you off. But I do have this atrocious itch.
(scratches more vigorously)

Godfrey: Are you itching for a fight?

Annesley: Itching? I've bathed recently. You
might look into one yourself.

Sanderson: We've got baths on our ship.

Captain makes sure ours is just as good as
yours.

Annesley: But not better.

Sanderson: Yo.

Enter Bostock

Godfrey: (Whispering so only Sanderson hears)
Tell him "better". Here comes Cap's man.

Sanderson: (to Annesley) I'd go with better,
man.

Annesley: Sucking lies through your teeth will
leave you in dentures.

Sanderson: If you got more than one knife on
you and keep it sharp, pull the sharp one,
Godfrey. I hope you're just as good at
thrusting it as the blunt one.

They fight

Bostock: (Breaks up the fight, swords scattering
to the ground on both sides) Cool it, you
idiots. You wanna get both of us under Gov's
nose?

Enter Tyndall

Tyndall: You'd chip your blade against mere
crew, Bostock. Here, turn around and let me
show you what a proper fight looks like.

Bostock: You're not helping here, Tyndall. Help
me get these clam brains to put their blades
away.

Tyndall: You want my help? Here, let me help you and all the Montgomerys into the sea.

Montgomery and Lutterell crews join in on the scuffle
Enter several Market Watch with muskets

First Market Watch: We've had it with you pirates, Blades and Albatrosses both. To arms, men; cock and ready on my signal.

Enter Captain Lutterell in regalia with Sailing Master Luther

Captain Lutterell: Luther, where's my sword? This'll be great exercise.
Sailing Master Luther: Maybe gentle yoga would be better, sir. Doc will scream at you if you throw your back again. Why a sword of all things?

Enter Captain Montgomery with rapier and Sailing Master Monsell with cutlass drawn

Captain Lutterell: Because that pampered hen is here, and she's got her little fencing blade out just 'cause she knows it pisses me off when people use those things.
Captain Montgomery: Lutterell, you eel shit. (Sailing Master Monsell stalls her) You'd best get your hand off my shoulder, Monsell.
Sailing Master Monsell: Don't lower yourself to an eel shit, Monty.

Enter Governor with community leaders

Governor: (shouting at the crews and citizens)
Freaking pirates! This is why we can't get
reasonable shipping here. You two (points at
Montgomery and Lutterell), gain control of
your men. Third time I've been summoned
to break up one of your men's rows because
you two fight like cats and dogs. The Market
Watch is sick of it. You can pay all your
portage fees and taxes on time, better than
many, but if I have to break this up again,
you're getting strung up where you can't
trouble the good people again.

Exeunt all but Montgomery, Monsell, and Bostock

Captain Montgomery: Bostock. Speak plain.
What the fuck?
Bostock: Uh...? Well, you know Lutterell. Your
crew was kicking his crew's asses. Which
would have been nice, other than we were
already on strike three with Gov, so figured I
probably needed them to quit it. Then Tin-
Tin shows up and just has to get involved.
And one thing led to another, and yeah...
Sailing Master Monsell: At least it all cooled off
before Roman showed up. Where is that
moonstruck calf of a nephew of mine?
Bostock: Off wallowing in self-pity on the dock-
side. Feeding seagulls.
Captain Montgomery: He's determined to
make the ocean saltier overnight. Then he
comes tumbling into the cabins at bloody
dawn without a thought to any of the crew

still sleeping. I don't mind him being a night owl, but it's getting worse if all he's doing is coming back and sleeping the day off. He'll never see daylight at this rate.

Bostock: Any idea why he's gone all mopey on us?

Captain Montgomery: Good question. No idea.

Bostock: Tried talking to him?

Captain Montgomery: Me, Sailing Master, Josephina, the crew. Even tried getting him wasted at Madam Linley's. He's determined to be his own best friend, and quite honestly, if you aren't nice to yourself, being your own best friend might be akin to being your own worst enemy. If you can pry it out of him, by all means, enlighten the rest of us. I need my quartermaster back to normal.

Enter Roman

Bostock: (cracking knuckles) Speaking of the overseer of hell. Let me have a go at him. I'll crack him like a bivalve.

Captain Montgomery: Good luck. Bring him back in one piece. Ice and whiskey, depending on who needs what, will be available if you can actually get him to talk. Come on, Monsell.

Exeunt Captain Montgomery and Sailing Master Monsell

Bostock: What are you building this time, Rome?

Roman: Oh, jeez, it's too early for this again, Bostock.

Bostock: Says the guy who's been up since the moon rose.

Roman: Meh. Just have a lot of things on my mind. Something happen for Monty and Monsell to be here?

Bostock: They're just off for a wander. Back to you, though, O king of the dark. What's troubling your tide pools?

Roman: If only I could stop the tides from rolling.

Bostock: Dude, you sound seasick.

Roman: Sick, maybe.

Bostock: Sick of love?

Roman: Maybe it's masochistic.

Bostock: She a complete dom?

Roman: There's this whole euphoria thing with this love at first sight business, and I'm just over here tired of being in it. (Sees signs of scuffle). A fight? Again? For the third time? Blades and Albatrosses just love themselves a good fight. Ironic, in a way. A love like that, don't you think?

Bostock: Alright, Aristotle, when'd you turn from quartermaster to philosopher? I think that entails a pay cut.

Roman: You're having a go at me.

Bostock: Dude, you're deep diving on irony when it was just another crew spat because you're all mopey about a pair of legs.

Roman: You ever been in love, Bostock? Straight up, it's madness. Everything is a knife's edge over an abyss. Especially when it's a stupid one-sided crush. I should get going.

Bostock: Hold up, turtle dove. You can't leave me hanging on this.

Roman: I haven't been myself in a while, Bos. Feels like my brain checked out and has been circling the stars while my body and simpler thoughts are stuck here waiting for me to return.

Bostock: Seriously, who the hell are you so gaga over that you're spouting romantics and philosophy?

Roman: You really want to know? You're just going to use it to tease me more.

Bostock: I'll keep the teasing to the minimum if it's worth it.

Roman: You have to promise on the captain's rapier you won't tease me for this. I can't take that at the moment.

Bostock: On her rapier, I promise.

Roman: She's not a dom. He's handsome to a fault.

Bostock: Then he must be a star.

Roman: A star would make the most sense of this situation I find myself in. You can reach for a star, use it to navigate by, admire it, and yet it will always be so distant from those of us who find ourselves swayed instead by an unrelenting sea on a deck too small.

Bostock: Then he finds himself amongst unreachable stars?

Roman: Those who flit around him are themselves bound to the heavens, far above the reach of us mere mortals.

Bostock: If they occupy the heavens, and you occupy the seas, then find someone of the seas. Poseidon, Lir, Njord may occupy the heavens and yet found themselves overseers of our waves.

Roman: How do I move on from a star, from this fellow Bastion?

Bostock: By setting your telescope a little closer to the deck. There must be ones circling your orbit.

Roman: To lower my scope would only remind me of what I saw before me. Handsome men around here have a terrible tendency of wearing eye masks and becoming some swashbuckling loners thinking they'll make a crew for themselves, and then you never hear from them again. No. Show me someone really up there, and then maybe I'd listen.

Bostock: You're on.

Exeunt Bostock and Roman

SCENE 2

SQUANDERER'S BAY: IN THE MARKET

Enter Captain Lutterell, Captain Parker, and Palmer

Captain Lutterell: (mid-conversation) Damn it. It's the tradition of the thing. Yet, if we are to maintain our port of call in the Bay, the fighting has to stop. Montgomery agreed to the truce with Gov. I didn't think she would, quite honestly.

Captain Parker: Privateers for the same crown, after all. I don't see why keeping a truce will be difficult. This will benefit all of us. Speaking of benefits: are you still thinking of shifting management? I am keen on the idea of obtaining a quartermaster with decent experience.

Captain Lutterell: Though your proposition from before is still remembered, I will say it: they've had a rough time of the last few months. Got caught up in crossfire. Lost an eye for the last good haul we had. Give them some more time to find themself before hoping they'll ship out with a new captain, crew, and ship.

Captain Parker: Men have suffered worse afflictions and been able to return to their post faster.

Captain Lutterell: I leave it up to them and you then. If they decide to join up with your crew, congratulations on encouraging them to face the seas again. I'd suggest tact, or else they'll never talk to you again. Says you me, the crew and I are having a party at the Prodigal Son on Speculate Lane near The Black Albatross's dock. Come down. Share a toast or two and maybe see what they make of you. We've got others of the Crown contract coming. Silver Turtle, Amethyst Harpoon, and a few others. Maybe talk to those quartermasters and see if any of them would be a better fit for your voyage. (to Palmer, giving a paper) Here's a list of other people outside of the contract I want to have show up tonight. They're at some of the south and north docks, and I haven't taken time to wander all the way out there. Take a quick jaunt and send them our way, would you? Thanks.

Exeunt Captain Lutterell and Captain Parker

Palmer: Frickin' fab, Cap. I could reef a sail for you, but no. I could stitch it, but no. I can even cook, not as great as Cook's, but no. Instead, you go handing me a paper

knowing damn well I can't read. Or at least
you would know if you'd remember my
name, you weather-beaten old sea turtle.
Oh, thank Poseidon's shiny trident, people
who look like they might know what this
scribbledy gook is.

Enter Bostock and Roman

Bostock: (to Roman) Bitter things can make
your stomach hurt, and yet the doc gives you
bitter things to make your stomach stop
hurting. A hot knife to a pussed wound
burns as bad as when you got the wound,
but it cures it. What you need for your
lovesick moonstruck calf face is a new beau
to look at. You need a different crush by
which to feel crushed over, then you can
forget about the last one that left you feeling
all bruised.

Roman: Hot water bottle is good for that.

Bostock: For what?

Roman: For a bruise.

Bostock: Roman, where is your head at?

Roman: Somewhere in a cloud nine restricted
zone, and I'm not sure if I want to stay in or
come out.

(to Palmer) Hi. You look a bit lost. Can I help?

Palmer: Oh, thank God, yes. Can you read?

Roman: I used to read between the lines, but I
think that has become lost on me.

Palmer: Not quite the skill I had in mind. Can
you read common words?

Roman: Yep. Several languages, to be a little less vague.

Palmer: That's still more vague than specific. I'll just, um...go...

Roman: Hold up, hold up. Let me see the paper. I'll see if I can help. (Takes list from Palmer) Uh. Okay, wait a minute. Where'd you get this? From a chicken? Horrid handwriting. You've got Captain Mario from Shrieking Badger, his quartermaster and sailing master and three guests over at Dock B9. Captain Allard of The Djinn's Lamp and her wife on Dock C7. Late Captain Vinny's husband who has residence with the Lagoon Maiden crew on Dock 2A. Sir Reginald with his Majesty's service located in South Docks, Cat's Eye pier. My brother Sir Lutterell with His Majesty's service in South Docks, Beryl pier. My nephew Bastion and his girl...oh...girlfriend of Seething Ghost. Sir Sigfried and Tyndall, they'll be at Wind-divers Lane and Hana of Vermillion Wave. That is quite a list. Know where you're sending them?

Palmer: Food.

Roman: Ah, a meal?

Palmer: Party at Prodigal Son for us.

Roman: Us?

Palmer: Captain.

Roman: Would make sense. I should have asked before who they were.

Palmer: Oh, right. I was being vague, sorry. Captain Lutterell. With so many people showing up, as long as you aren't from The Crimson Blade, I'd think Captain wouldn't mind you slipping in. Not like he notices much anyway. He can't ever remember I can't read. Probably doesn't even remember my name most days. Anyway. I gotta get. Peace.

Exit Palmer

Bostock: Bastion's gonna be at Prodigal Son? Like, the Bastion guy you're all mopey over? And girlfriend. That's gotta suck. But. Wait, Roman. Hear me out. You saw that list there. Not everyone on it revolves in the heavens like old Bass boy. What say you to us going and taking our pick of the litter, hmm?

Roman: No one there will ever compare to him.

Bostock: Let me guess. He was rigging a ship all on his lonesome out at the dock, and no one was around, and you just swooned over a pair of good arms. There are other great arms around here, or else there would be no good crew in all of Squanderer's Bay.

Roman: Well...um...Let's crash Prodigal Son. Not because I think you're right. You have to see this guy. I know, not your type, but maybe you'll get where I'm coming from.

Exeunt Roman and Bostock

SCENE 3

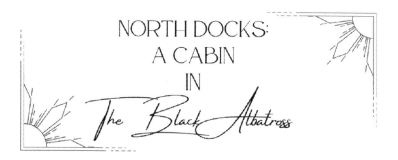

NORTH DOCKS: A CABIN IN *The Black Albatross*

Enter Sailing Master Luther and Doc

Sailing Master Luther: Are they doing better? It's been three months.

Doc: I'll go call them. They're in the next cabin over.

Exit Doc

Enter Doc and Jules

Jules: I'm awake. Maybe with a migraine, but I am currently occupying the land of the living.

Doc: Well, that's a relief. Would rather not have a wraith walking around the ship.

Jules: Luther? How can I help you?

Sailing Master Luther: Not sure if you need to be here for this, Doc. Probably wouldn't hurt either way.

Doc: I can leave.

Sailing Master Luther: No, stay. It's alright. Just

debating on how to put this. They'll never
recover their eye, will they?

Doc: If you were to find a magic potion in the
Lighthouse at the end of the world, maybe.
Being realistic, though... no, it's clean gone.

Sailing Master Luther: Why would the Lighthouse have magical potions?

Doc: Why else would it be shrouded in
perpetual darkness? Hearsay says there's a
stone lantern that, upon being lit by an
impossible fuel, will lift the darkness and
return the island to its rightful place in the
world. Superstition has it that the Lighthouse was cursed by an angry goddess when
the Lighthouse keeper, who had devoted
himself to the discovery of the alchemical
Rebis, concluded that his light could be used
in achieving his goal of surpassing the
known world.

Sailing Master Luther: And this intrinsically
means that the Lighthouse has magic eye
potions?

Doc: Well, probably not, but The Black Albatross
has crossed dangerous oceans for more
mysterious and marvellous things, and they
be true.

Jules: I'm not so bent out of shape about my lost
eye as to travel to the Lighthouse, Doc. We
can leave off on the fairy tales for a bit.

Doc: If you aren't interested in magically
poofing your pretty eye back into existence,
then hear me out. I want access to the guy's
medicine cabinet. Elixirs and potions are one

thing. The base components used in many alchemical practices are fundamental to real medicine, and it would be nice to fill my larder.

Sailing Master Luther: Noted about the medicine cabinet, Doc. I'll have a word with Captain. As it is, Captain will be having a word with you, Jules, about the fact that Parker is after you to be his quartermaster.

Jules: To change contracts is not one of my personal motivations in life.

Doc: No ambitions for a raise?

Sailing Master Luther: We've been docked bayside for three months getting you back to normal.

Doc: "Normal" does not entirely define what is going on here, Luther. As it is, you all had cargo to unload from that haul out of Coralie de Couer. Silver and silks from Carteen are not easily come by. Though their shipspeople most certainly are, and good shots, mind you.

Sailing Master Luther: And now the silk has been sold, and we're sitting on funds for our next run waiting. Return to work, Jules. Whether that be with the Albatross or someone else. It would be better than squandering your life in a dark hole because you lost a bit of your eyesight. You need a deviation. Something interesting.

Doc: I mean, the guy recruiting isn't known to be a straight-up arse, so it might not be a lousy deviation from the usual.

Sailing Master Luther: (to himself) I hate this potential contract upheaval.

Doc: (to Jules) Taking on a different contract might let you see more than the little triangle we run.

Sailing Master Luther: (to Jules) Is that a yes to getting back to being our quartermaster or a yes to joining up with the new crew?

Jules: It's not like I want to leave the Albatross. I'm just, well, a bit gun-shy at the moment. It'll get better. Don't go tossing me to another crew just because you think I'm unhappy here. I'll be unhappy there too, and for the same reason.

Enter Palmer

Palmer: Sailing Master, Doc, Quartermaster, the guests are arriving, and Captain wants you down there, NOW!

Sailing Master Luther: Oh, blast it all. Jules, figure it out. Are you staying as our quartermaster or hiring on with a new contract? Because one way or another, your talent needs to stop being wasted in a medical bay.

Doc: Come on, Jules, let's follow them. Luther isn't wrong. It'd help you to get back into work rather than lying about down here.

Exeunt all

SCENE 4

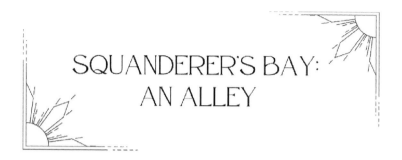

SQUANDERER'S BAY: AN ALLEY

Enter Roman, Bostock, and Malone, all disguised as theatrical performers of Hamlet for the pub stage

Roman: So, we just going in like this? We supposed to introduce ourselves or what?

Bostock: Nothing extreme. These types of pub performances, half the time you're lucky to leave the stage without tomato on your face. Just get up and act. Don't worry about us being a "troop" or a "band" or something for people to "find" us by later.

Roman: Can I be the king? I don't want to say lines. Let me just sleep and die, please?

Malone: Hah. You wish. You're the only one of the crew who has the entirety of Shakespeare memorised down to the stage exits. Like hell are we letting you be the backdrop.

Roman: You just want to hear my voice crack.

Malone: It'll be better than the nine troy ounces of cracked gold you've got in that chest of yours.

Roman: And is it ever a heavy weight to carry.

Malone: What you need is to patch that lead-shot filled heart before it sinks you in Davy's locker.

Roman: He may not make for bad company.

Malone: For now, though, pick up that burdensome heart, and put on your mask. You're in our company for the time being, and maybe we'll find someone to unload the buckshot from your feels.

Bostock: Come on, slowpokes, we need to get in there.

Roman: Seriously though, let me be the king.

Malone: No can do, toucan. You do better performing than you do glooming about.

Roman: Maybe I should just play Hamlet and kill everyone.

Malone: As long as it doesn't get Monty down our throats.

Roman: This is a bad idea, not just me performing.

Malone: I think it's bloody brilliant.

Roman: I had this dream yesterday.

Malone: So did I. What a coincidence.

Roman: You gonna share your dream with the rest of the class?

Malone: Sure. I had to take over for Monty for a day and convinced the guys to take up a bit of fishing. We caught this monster of a shark that pulled us all in, and we found the largest pearls in an oyster bed and made bank. Only after we got ported did I find out I'd done the whole thing without my pants.

Now, which part of that dream is the biggest
fish story you ever heard?

Roman: Probably about the part where you
sleep long enough to have a dream.

Malone: Says the guy who's been watching
Selene drive her chariot across the sky a
week running now. One'd think you'd fallen
in love with her.

Roman: Maybe just hoping she'd give me a
couple words of wisdom.

Malone: Here's your words of wisdom then,
lover boy: loosen the hell up. We're just
gonna have a bit of fun.

Bostock: Y'all keep yammering, and we'll never
get there in time. They've already finished
doing rounds on meals. I see the waiters
clearing out the first round of trash bins for
the evening.

Roman: This has got me all kinds of vibes. An
enriching experience that'll leave me poorer
in the end. Or maybe a poor experience
leaving me richer in the end. An odd feeling.
I guess I must be odd if we're planning on
doing Hamlet in front of Lutterell.

Bostock: Put on a bit o'swagger, boys. We're
going in.

Exeunt Roman, Bostock, and Malone

SCENE 5

SQUANDERER'S BAY: PRODIGAL SON

Musicians waiting
Enter pub staff with help from Galley crew

> **Palmer**: Damn it all, where'd that bilge rat get off to? I can't have plates stacking up here.
>
> **Galley Help**: Help, good or otherwise, is almost impossible these days.
>
> **Palmer**: Jefferson! Show yourself, you sodding clot! Louis, take this crap out of here before I knock something over. Leave me a bit of that pie if you know what's good for you.
>
> **Galley Help**: On it, sir!
>
> **Jefferson**: What! What! What! I'm here.
>
> **Palmer**: Cap's looking for you.
>
> **Galley Help**: You can't be both here and with the Cap. Get out of here!

Exeunt Palmer and Jefferson

Enter Captain Lutterell, Boatswain, Tyndall, Sailing Master Luther,

Jules, and other crew members. Black Albatross crew meet Roman,
Bostock, Malone, other party members, and pub staff

Captain Lutterell: Welcome, crew and friends
of The Black Albatross! We celebrate tonight!
Though it is not of tradition to keep the
times in such a manner, I wish you to join
me in marking the passing of my seventy-
fifth year alive and fiftieth year as captain of
The Black Albatross! I must blame my luck
on Fortuna and the madams of the Bay!
Now, behold, entertainment of a type for the
evening. Food, drink, crappy actors. Who
brought the tomatoes? Right. Boatswain!
Bring the box over here and sit down. You
and I are gonna see who gets the first actor
in the face. (Sits down in chair).

Boatswain: (brings box of rotting tomatoes and
sets it next to Captain's chair before sitting
down). Best seat in the house, Captain. You
always remember my arthritis.

Captain Lutterell: Surely you can't be arthritic,
you old gunner. You're just fifteen years my
younger.

Boatswain: You keep adding to that number,
Cap. I'm five years your younger, and we
grew up chasing seagulls not far from our
mothers' skirts.

Captain Lutterell: You were chasing seagulls. I
was chasing skirts.

Roman: (whispering to a crewman, pointing out
Jules) Psst. Yeah, you. Hey, who's that over
there? No, not that one. The one with the

eyepatch. Oye, no, my blind fellow. Okay, fair, half the people here have one. Yes, you've got one, I get it. Sorry. The one with the bit of swagger. Yeah, yeah, that one.

Crewman: No clue.

Roman: Damn.

Tyndall: I smell a Montgomery. (to a crewman) I left my knife in my cabin. Bring it to me. No one of the Blade curses my crew.

Captain Lutterell: Tyndall, what, by all the pearls in the hold, are you going on about?

Tyndall: We've got a Blade in here. They've come to crash the party.

Captain Lutterell: Hold, Tyndall. It's Roman, isn't it, under that costume? Good Lord, he's dressed as Hamlet.

Tyndall: An even worse omen. Let me spill his guts across the deck.

Captain Lutterell: No, don't go slicing him apart. Even the Blade can spit out decent people. He's upstanding to a fault and has no stomach for bloodletting. He's their quarter-master, and we might just have need to split him from the Blade if'n our Jules takes up with Captain Parker's crew instead.

Tyndall: You cannot be serious, sir.

Captain Lutterell: You want to test that accusa-tion, Tyndall?

Tyndall: You would protect a Montgomery after everything they've done to us?

Captain Lutterell: Shut it, Tyndall. Last warn-ing. Don't jeopardise the truce. It's tenuous as it is. He's known as one of the most

virtuous of the quartermasters in these
parts.

Tyndall: Have it your way. His being here is just
asking for the crew to go volatile, and then
we really will have Montgomery up our
mast.

Exit Tyndall

Roman: (Sips beer before approaching Jules.
Offers Jules the pint.) Bit lonely over here,
don't you think?

Jules: (Takes beer) They say sharing a glass
someone's drank from is like a second-hand
kiss. (Drinks)

Roman: And your thoughts on second-hand
kisses?

Jules: I prefer them first-hand.

Roman: You seem not to mind a second-hand
kiss from me.

Jules: It is not so much that I do not mind.

Roman: Then, will you mind first-hand?

Jules: Only if you don't free me of this whole
flirting thing. I'm crap at this.

Roman: Then allow me a liberty. (They kiss.) Ale
does taste better this way if I might say so.

Jules: I might agree.

Roman: Would you like to be certain?

Jules: If you would like to be sure. (They kiss
once more.) Even bad pick-up lines yield
good results some days.

Doc: Quartermaster, Sailing Master wants you.

Jules moves to leave

Roman: Who is their Sailing Master?

Doc: Luther from the Albatross.

Roman: May they fly and never land.

(To himself) Crap, an Albatross. What bad luck does Fortuna wish to bless me with this time?

Bostock: Let's get out before you have to mono-logue more Hamlet. They've got tomatoes, and they're throwing them at both the good and bad acts.

Roman: I'd brave the tomatoes.

Captain Lutterell: Now, now, my fine actors, don't exit stage left just yet! I promise to withhold the tomatoes if you give us another glimpse into the life of Hamlet! (pub staff whispers in his ear) Past hours! It was just getting fun. Fine. Alright, you bilge rats, return to your stations. We're getting evicted for the favour of the rising sun.

Exeunt all but Jules and Doc

Jules: Doc, my vision isn't what it was. Who's that leaving?

Doc: One of the Shrieking Badger's gunners.

Jules: And that? They all look alike right now.

Doc: Let me think. The Djinn's Lamp's sailing master—or was she the quartermaster?

Jules: And the ones from the play tonight?

Doc: No clue, Jules. It's late. Or early. What is dawn when you've been up all night?

Jules: Go ask, I can't see in this glare, and I think Captain would like to see them do another play sometime. (Doc leaves) I might just have a celebrity crush now.

Doc: We had a freaking Montgomery in the house. Roman, their quartermaster, played Hamlet.

Jules: And he has good taste in beer.

Doc: Hold up. Do what?

Jules: Prodigal Son's stocking good beer.

(Someone calls for Jules from offstage)

Doc: It was stale. Let's get back to ship and get you reinstated in your regular cabin. It has a good vantage overlooking the fleets this time around. You've been in the infirmary since before we docked. Waking up to something nice to look at will be easy on the eye.

Exeunt all

ACT 2

PROLOGUE

PROLOGUE
Act 2

Enter Chorus

Chorus:
The Norns, capricious mistresses of time
Play sweet torment on Yggdrasil's frail limbs.
Love beneath its boughs on th'waves sublime,
Dangerous and yet beautiful whims,
Does Roman ponder from the ship's great deck.
An enchanting quartermaster's most ill fate:
An affection, stolen before 'tis met.
Treacherous, his contemplations of late:
That he would leave his captain for another
Only to see one fair as love itself.
And fair as love, Jules thinks of no other,
A shared kiss flavoured from the high shelf.
And that through fate they encounter once more
Whether that be on land or behind an oar.

Exeunt all

SCENE 1

ACT 2, SCENE 1

NORTH DOCKS:
WAREHOUSE
NEAR
The Black Albatross

Enter Roman

> **Roman:** I should be away from here. Yet my self-ishness drives me to glimpse a wonder more prized than mythical treasures.

Exit Roman
Enter Bostock and Malone

> **Bostock:** (calling Roman) Roman! Yo, Rome! Oye, Quartermaster!
> **Malone:** Probably got himself lost on these docks and wandered himself back homeward.
> **Bostock:** He's sensitive to the sun, the moon, the stars. He plots the universe in his head and can navigate with no map. He wouldn't get himself lost.
> **Malone:** You're not wrong. Maybe that lead-shot filled heart of his finally sank him beneath the waves. Shall I see if I can call his

ghost? Roman! Quartermaster Roman! Navigator of Kraken's Whirlpools! Explorer of the Great Blue Hole! Have you finally found a breaker reef you couldn't avoid? You hapless, lovestruck, calf-faced, turtledove, show yourself!

Bostock: You know he hates those nicknames.

Malone: They're true.

Bostock: And he has truly made himself scarce for the dawn. Let him admire Apollo's chariot. It seems to be the company he desires more right now.

Malone: Leave him to the sun, and he will wish Apollo hold him. What he needs is to visit with Linley and see if she has any fine beaus willing to play Apollo for a day or Eros a night. Come on, I'm tired and have to be up in a few hours to load up our necessities.

Bostock: You're not wrong on either front. Let him find himself either a sunburn on the sands or a trist by lamplight.

Exeunt Malone and Bostock

SCENE 2

ACT 2, SCENE 2

NORTH DOCKS: OUTSIDE
The Black Albatross

Enter Roman

Roman: Easy for him to say. He's never been burned.

Enter Jules on a private deck of the ship

Roman: Apollo would pale in comparison. Lamplight would be that of darkness in a storm at midnight. The stars surely would congregate, thinking the moon replaced. Would it be that Jules were the moon in the sky that I might see them every night. Yet, if they were the moon, I would be no more than a man reaching for the heavens. What says I, wishing to step into the realm of the cosmos if only to glimpse one blessed with the North Star for an eye? Enraptured with their gravity, I would wish not to travel the stars, but to be a planet, trapped within their orbital pull. They could still the tides and

end the winds, and yet I would stand upon
the deck of a motionless ship and praise
them for existing.

Jules: Oye.

Roman: (to himself) Their voice, like that of
Venus, of Parvati, of the universe itself.
Speak once more, if only that I may learn
what it is to stand so close to a holy blessing.

Jules: (not aware of Roman's presence) Roman.
Roman. I do not wish to see Rome burn
tonight. I wish for its resurgence, if not for
his Caesar. Would that Roman be instead
Gaul or Norse. Would that he might a new
leader elect. If no change is to be found, I
would become a citizen of his and forego
my own.

Roman: (to himself) To interrupt would break
this spell. Dare I hope for better?

Jules: (not aware of Roman's presence) Under
the same sky. Under the same country's flag.
And yet it is not you yourself that is what lies
between us but the ink on a contract. That it
belongs to a captain not my own. That my
own wars against yours. You are not your
captain, though. Neither I. Would that
instead we took ship and sailed. Saw the
stars beneath our own flag. We would
neither fear each other's contract, for ours
would be to each other.

Roman: (to Jules) If you speak truly, I would
quartermaster for you. I would break my
contract and no longer linger in the shadow
of the Montgomery flag.

Jules: Scare the stars out of starfish, mate! Where are you hiding?

Roman: Stuck behind a bunch of barrels, wondering how I might break a contract without breaking a heart.

Jules: Roman? Were you...? Did you hear all of that? Oh, that's embarrassing.

Roman: You and me both. Breathing poetics like fish gulping water. Aren't we both just dramatic?

Jules: What are you doing lingering around Lutterell's ship? You trying to get yourself shot?

Roman: I would face the end of a musket to see you again.

Jules: I can guarantee the rest of the crew does not want to see you.

Roman: But do you?

Jules: I—I... Yes?

Roman: Then whether they see me or not, I have seen paradise and know heaven is lesser than.

Jules: How'd you know this was my side of the ship?

Roman: You shine so bright. I would mark my backstaff by your passage. Across the ocean, and you would still draw me to you like a lodestone needle.

Jules: What would you call this, our infatuation?

Roman: Love.

Jules: Are your words as honest as they are simple?

Roman: More so than any treasure map shows the true location of its precious hoard.

Jules: Treasure maps are more often distractions than they are revealers of loot. I do not wish to only be a distraction, and I believe you do not wish to be yet another pirate on a failed hunt.

Roman: How should I promise they be honest and simple?

Jules: Do not promise. Promises are easily broken in the meanderment of time and whim. Prove them. That what we have here is more than a passing moment between two people bored from a party neither of us wished to attend.

Roman: Would that I could prove—

Jules: I would see you prove it, yes, but in turn, I would also, and in the end, we are as yet new to each other. This current is a bit too quick to navigate safely. Let us find the eddies, the calm sea, to learn how this ship sails.

Roman: Then we must find us some place by which to test how our canvas catches the line of the zephyr.

Jules: You are willing to seek out a safe harbour for us to investigate the waters beneath our bow?

Roman: For you, I would float through the darkness at the edge of the world and beyond to navigate the stars. I will call this love until my dying breath in the frozen wastes.

Jules: I would travel those seas with you if you

would have me. If you would take me for
what I am, blind by half.

Roman: Blind by half you might be, and that
may be why you don't see yourself the way I
see you. Sail with me as you are. I would be a
fool to turn you away for want of a bit of
depth perception.

Jules: And as I know of you, I'm informed that
you are not keen on blood or battle, rather an
unhurried existence of well-played acquisi-
tion to the chagrin of your captain. I think a
match we make.

Doc calls from off stage.

Jules: (to Roman) Looks like I'm being
summoned. What's your bet: cod-liver oil or
witch hazel? (to Doc) I'm coming back in,
just getting a breath of fresh air, Doc. (to
Roman) I should wish you goodbye now,
sweet Quartermaster. Hold for a minute,
though.

Exit Jules

Roman: Is this a dream? Surely it is not a nightmare, and I will wake in my berth.

Enter Jules

Jules: Cap's got some big announcement, so I
have to get. Before I go, though: if memory
recalls, our contracts with the Privateer

Offices of the Crown are void if our names change. What says you to finding us a priest? Send back word if you find a way and want to do this thing.

Doc (offstage): Quartermaster!

Jules: But if that is not quite your intention—

Doc (offstage): Jules Road, Cap's gonna have your hide!

Jules: That's not good.

(to Doc) Alright! Aye, right, man, I hear you!

(to Roman) I'll send a messenger. Let me know your reply.

Roman: My mooring depends on it.

Jules: Then check your line and make sure the knot doesn't slip.

Exit Jules

Roman: To leave you is like saying goodbye to the port with the one good cook, knowing you're on rations for a year. My stomach is knotted at the thought.

Roman goes to leave
Jules returns to the balcony

Jules: I dream already of the waves I will see with you. And I'm a better cook than you'll find at any port of call.

Roman: Then you must be home, for they say that home is where one wishes to always be.

Jules: Roman!

Roman: Yes, my chef?

Jules: When should I send the messenger?

Roman: Before the cock crows, lest there be someone in the nest watching.

Jules: Before the cock crows. That's not all I came out here for. Now, what was it?

Roman: I have all night to watch you think.

Jules: You will be standing there while the stars fall from the heavens at this rate. I have enjoyed your company, though, and hope to enjoy more.

Roman: Let them fall while you remember; it is a beautiful view.

Jules: It grows much too late already. The stars are almost disappearing. That I would catch one and give it to you to light your way back.

Roman: I would rather be the star you caught.

Jules: And yet a star dies out, and I would never want your shine to fade. A diamond you are, forever and casting a sparkle as dazzling. Goodnight, my sweet gem.

Exit Jules

Roman: That I was your gem, worn on your ear where I could whisper sweetness to lay you to sleep. I shall seek out one who might know a way of breaking contracts, though, so that I need not be the gem on your ear at night but one to share your world with you hand in hand.

Exit Roman

SCENE 3

ACT 2, SCENE 3

NORTH DOCKS: MADAM LINLEY'S BROTHEL SHIP
The Red Lantern

Enter Madam Linley carrying an armload of dresses

Madam Linley: Washing. Cleaning. Cooking. Mending. Caring. One would think I was a housekeeper, not a Madam. The ship needs its upkeep, though. Always does. Always will. We are called a great many a name on board this ship, in each berth and hallway, sweet and surly both. One might say we have no virtue. One might turn around and call us saints. In the end, we're all just trying to get by. Can vice become virtue? Would the woman who steals a loaf of bread be in the wrong for feeding her child? What of those discouraged from feeding the homeless who do so regardless of the fines? And this is what I get: musings to the universe when I do not wish to pick up the needle and thread in such dim lamplight. Never-ending, isn't it? The work. I get up and work. I lie down and work. I sleep and dream of work.

Enter Roman with carafe

Madam Linley: When am I not working, I ask
you? I am a captain of this entire ship, and
yet I am perpetually at the beck and call of
every other living soul on this entire planet.
May I someday have dry land and a little
cabin in which to rest my weary bones. Give
those who keep the rooms a place where
they can enjoy paradise, rather than
providing paradise.

Roman: May I witness this paradise, the one you
would enjoy instead of the one everyone
enjoys?

Madam Linley: Roman! What are you doing flit-
ting about my decks at who knows how late
in the evening? A paradise, I tell you! One
that lies to the south and west. An island on
which there are mild summers and warm
winters. A freshwater source from an ice-
cold lake. Where the fruit of the trees is so
cumulous we would never hunger. I would
give away my ship the day we had houses
there beneath the canopies. I know, though,
you fiend of a navigator, that if I showed you
my map, you'd remember it until the day
you died. Not to say you aren't welcome
there, but I would rather the rest of the
crews in the area didn't know of it. It is late
enough that the patrons have all returned to
their own beds, and yet here you stand, looking—for want of a better word—lovestruck.

Roman: You are not entirely wrong with your description.

Madam Linley: Not one of the lilies on board The Red Lantern, I should hope. You will not hear the end of it from me if one of them ends up teary-eyed over you when you ship out again. Then again. You've never taken a berth on this ship. All you do is come bearing cold tea and seek out a few hours of simple talk with whoever will listen to you muse about the turnings of the world.

Roman: No. No, I'm not one for plucking lily petals from someone else's garden, even a community garden. It would only lead to sadness, knowing the flower was not truly mine alone to adore.

Madam Linley: Then have you found a lily for your garden? Or are you here to muse about something else?

Roman: How I wish it were something else to muse upon. It would save me what I know will be torment. I've been drinking in a garden not my own. There a lily lies: a star fallen to earth. I have gazed upon it, and in so doing, wish to acquire it, but find the prospect difficult. You see, it is owned by someone who is none too pleased with the one who owns me. Though I wish to be planted near this stargazer lily, it would seem it could only benefit one or the other, and that would lead to trouble. Cultivator of lilies, would you be able to transplant us such that neither owner is slighted by the other?

Madam Linley: Alright, drop the metaphor.

Roman: You know how Captain Lutterell and Captain Montogomery hate each other? Yeah. I've fallen in love with Lutterell's quartermaster. And they me. And, well, neither captain will marry us, probably. I'm not exactly excited by the idea of asking. You're a captain, and a third party who's always accommodated my need to just talk to someone. Could you marry us? I'd pay. I have coin for it. If done by a captain other than our own, the name change would break our contracts, and then we aren't making a mess for either of our captains. Privateer code, we don't need permission from our commanding officer. Just provide a letter of reason after the fact. The fear is: if either of us is seen together without that protection, then either Jules's captain or mine will go on a warpath. Is there any way to do it today?

Madam Linley: You? The one who pines over unattainable loves? What changed for you to go out of your way to actually talk to someone long enough to think this is love? I thought you were infatuated with some prick of a wannabe captain, last I heard from one of my lilies. Are you really ready to be in this kind of love? Or are you just in lust? There is a difference. And though one can lead to the other, you do not want to be trapped in legalities if it doesn't.

Roman: Would you like me to continue coming to the ship and waxing lyrics?

Madam Linley: When's the ceremony set for?

Roman: I am pained by such a quick response. Am I truly so despicable for contemplating the realities of life? I do pay for the time I waste of your lilies by existing as I am and do not fuss with their petals. It is not in my nature or interest.

Madam Linley: I would encourage you some dalliances with petals, if only to put your head on right in knowing the difference between a passing interest, an infatuation, and a firmly established relationship.

Roman: And yet the idea of dalliances has never appealed to me. I will love beauty upon the eyes. Any lily can be such. It is the petal, though, I have never touched, the interest never there. This once, though, I have smelled its perfume and desire to caress its creamy nature. This, it is more than I have experienced. I am sick with it and wish a cure. One that cannot be found in other gardens.

Madam Linley: Oh jeez, you really are in love, and not just an aesthetic infatuation. Yes. I'll help you with a ceremony. Keep you from being sick in love, and maybe get your captains to both shove their differences overboard.

Roman: Then you'll do it?

Madam Linley: Yes, yes, my pure man. Let's go see about transplanting a lily bulb, now that

you have found one whose soft petals you
wish to test.

Exeunt Roman and Madam Linley

SCENE 4

NORTH DOCKS:
OUTSIDE OF
The Crimson Blade

Enter Bostock and Malone

Malone: Did that astronomer ever return last
night? I thought we had cured him of his
moonlight wanderings.

Bostock: None of the rest of the crew has lantern
light or scope upon him either.

Malone: Is he still hung up over that Bastion
fellow? The guy up and left on his dinghy of
a ship and dumped his girlfriend all in one
day in order to "find himself." Roman needs
to get over this crush fast.

Bostock: A letter arrived on Monty's desk from
Old Tin-Tin.

Malone: What is Tyndall doing sending letters
to Monty? She'd rather skin him than be
near him. Oh, I'd bet you it's a duel. That's
probably what he's after.

Bostock: Roman will take the duel if he hears
word that Monty's been challenged. At least
then we'd know where he is for once.

Malone: Any of the men on ship would take up the duel for Monty. However, she'd beat all their asses for trying it.

Bostock: Roman would answer the challenge still. Monty saved him from a deserted island when his last crew abandoned him for being who he is. He's overprotective of her for it.

Malone: This is one challenger with whom he does not wish to cross swords.

Bostock: Tyndall that good?

Malone: He's the reason that old sea turtle of a captain of theirs is still as powerful as he was fifty years ago. Not like Lutterell can adequately wield a sword now. Who do you think does it in his place?

Bostock: He's the Scythe in the Albatross nest?

Malone: He's the Grim Reaper with the Albatross as his familiar.

Enter Roman

Bostock: Oye, Roman's showed up!

Malone: He looks ragged. Would that I never face a love as strained as his. I would not survive the night.

(to Roman) Roman! What bloody well took you so long? Plotting the course of the moon again?

Roman: Its course has already been plotted, better than I ever will. Why would I waste that kind of time?

Malone: If you weren't plotting courses, then why'd you ditch us last night?

Roman: It wasn't that I was ditching you. Maybe I was plotting courses other than the moon's path through heaven's waves.

Malone: I would be wary of any course leading to Ogygia. You might enjoy it for a time, but even Odessyus found its pleasures to fade.

Roman: I don't think I have ever seen it on any map I am familiar with.

Malone: That is probably for the better, then.

Roman: Though it sounds like you have experienced this Ogygia and learned a few lessons from it.

Malone: I find myself visiting on a whim, but nowhere to leave my anchor for longer than an evening's passage.

Roman: A passage for a passage.

Malone: So to speak.

Roman: Why then can you not tell your headings?

Malone: When you have been granted passage so often, why learn your headings? Just follow where it leads, and miracles await.

Roman: Come, it will be a miracle if this ends soon.

Malone: Bostock! Save us from these choppy waters.

Roman: Bailing so soon?

Malone: If I continue, you'll sink my ship for every loaded word you utter.

Roman: How much basalt must I add to your ballast? Surely it is already under the Plimsoll line.

Malone: Beware—my cannons are quicker loaded than your musket.

Roman: And yet my sharp cuts faster.

Malone: And now I am wounded. Leave me here to bleed out.

Roman: Adding blood to the water will only float my ship higher.

Malone: You're already too high. Maybe I'll staunch the holes you've left in me.

Roman: But I was just beginning to enjoy the view from the top.

Malone: It is a sight better for a view to be radiant against those eyes so downcast for so long. It appears that you have moved your ship from a bay never willing to let your ship dock.

Bostock: Let's not add wind to that sail.

Malone: You want me to cast anchor before reaching our destination?

Bostock: You will run us aground.

Malone: You do not trust the length of my chain and my knowledge of these depths.

Enter Doc with Palmer

Roman: This should be interesting.

Bostock: What have we here, a walking crow's nest?

Malone: A barrel man and a crow's nest by which to perch.

Doc: Cabin boy!

Palmer: Here, Doc.

Doc: Do you have that list I gave you?

Malone: Pray, good cabin boy, tell me the list is not as long as the writer.

Doc: I would say good morning, but good is questionable with you in it.

Malone: I mean, if it was u, it would not be spelt with two o's, then it would not be questionable.

Doc: It is too early in the morning for this.

Malone: It is nearly brunch, Doctor.

Doc: That is yet still too early to be dealing with this.

Malone: But not so early as to make other dealings?

Doc: Oh, my fracking... Get off with you.

Malone: That's what they all say in the end.

Doc: And they come to me complaining for it. Now lay off. Where can I find Roman?

Roman: Have I aged such that I am now a ghost, unrecognisable as my younger self?

Doc: I fear we will all be ghosts at this rate.

Malone: May we all lay in graves with smiles on our faces.

Doc: (to Roman) Is he always like this? You're Roman, right? Might I have a moment of your time while you are not a ghost?

Bostock: He will take more than just a moment, Roman.

Malone: I'm not certain Roman should refuse, then.

Roman: I have been given no reason to refuse.

Malone: Though I would have expected you to be happier letting a morning dove take more time than a grave man.

(singing)

legends old
graves grow cold
but their knowledge most sublime
the young are better
quite a bit fresher
but it all depends on taste

(speaking) We have brunch plans at Lucky Lady.
Are you coming, Roman?

Roman: If I did, what use would I be for the rest
of the day?

Malone: About as much use as the rest of us
once satisfied.

Exit Bostock and Malone

Doc: There's some talent in being able to talk
from both sides of the mouth.

Roman: He is one of those few capable of saying
more in the time passed by the minute hand
than the hour.

Doc: I'm not sure if I feel older for having kept
up with him or for having had my age
pointed out. (to Palmer) Am I a creaking bag
of bones, Palmer?

Palmer: You're three decades younger than
Captain, sir. I believe that makes you middle
age, not old.

Doc: That still stings. (to Roman) Now, my good

man. May I call you man, or would you
another? No? Alright, my good man. I have been
sent to find you because my quartermaster has
gotten it in their head that there is some
emotional connection between you two. Before
I go into what they had to say, let me speak my
peace. You ever make them cry, I will freaking
bury you where Davy Jones knows not. Got it?

Roman: I would expect nothing less than a
potter's field.

Doc: They're enamoured with you, and I cannot
see it as healthy, but to see them happy in
three months since losing their eye, I will not
begrudge possibly unwise choices such as
this.

Roman: You have spoken to them at length,
then. Are they truly happy with this plan?

Doc: The first time I think I've ever seen them
smile in the ten years they've served on ship
since coming to us as a cabin child at not less
than fourteen. Who knew it would take a
Montgomery quartermaster to split those
lips?

Roman: Is there a way for them to escape from
duties for a time to meet me at The Red
Lantern with their contract? This evening?
Can they find a way to do that? The Madam
has agreed to see us married and change our
contracts for us. (giving Doc a handful of
coins) For the trouble this is probably
causing you.

Doc: I can't.

Roman: You've had to travel to the docks and sacrifice time from your work.

Doc: (taking the coins) If you are determined, I will see they have their excuse to make it.

Roman: Linger in the stalls of the far market near your docking. I'll send a powder monkey to you with a bag for Jules as a gift for this evening.

Doc: You've heard what loose lips do.

Roman: They will not sink this ship.

Doc: Are you certain?

Roman: More so than the North Star hangs in the sky regardless of the cloud.

Doc: They speak of you in terms of diamonds. I hope you do not prove to be cut glass.

Roman: Even cut glass will sparkle; some will even carry a tune.

Doc: Some are more precious than a gem with an inclusion that will split the edge.

Roman: Tell Jules I look forward to seeing them again.

Doc: Ready to get back, Palmer?

Palmer: My feet are killing me. Yes.

Doc: I still have so much on that list to go source. (points to the list Palmer is holding)

Exeunt all

SCENE 5

NORTH DOCKS: JULES'S CABIN ON *The Black Albatross*

Enter Jules

Jules: Why does time have to seep like a tarless hull when important things are at hand? Where'd they get themselves off to looking for Roman? Have they lost the road? I need to be looking over course headings, acting normal. How am I supposed to act normal when my heart is unfurling like a sail in a warm breeze pointing me to the horizon? The waters are calm, and yet the deck heaves beneath my feet.

Enter Doc and Palmer

Jules: May Euphrosyne smile upon you. What have you found? Palmer, it's crowded in here with more than another. Mind waiting outside?

Doc: Sorry, cabin boy. Thank you.

Exit Palmer

Jules: You look glum. What happened?

Doc: I got called old. So, I'm feeling my years.

Jules: If I were old enough to be on the other
side of the news you bear, I might feel more.

Doc: Let me sit, let me sit. No one had what I
needed in the market today, and I am worn.

Jules: Sit, then, so that I can have my news.

Doc: You sure know how to pick them. What
was it that drew you to him? His seething
wit or his slashing eyes? I dare say he is
polite within reason, but a rogue is not what
you wish for. You're old enough to plot your
own courses. He seems keen on helping you
do so. I was out most of the morning. Have
you eaten?

Jules: Do you think I have an appetite right now?
It is easier to plot those courses with a quartermaster if I know I have one. What has he
said?

Doc: Why must my shoulders ache so much?
And my head? You'd think I was hungover
for having not touched a drop in years.
Maybe I should check myself into the infirmary. But who would then be a doctor if the
doctor has taken ill?

Jules: (rubs Doc's shoulders) For the bloody love
of all that is holy: speak, old man, before I
shake you apart.

Doc: You wouldn't dare.

Jules: My world is close to being shaken apart,
and I will take you with me if you keep it up.

Doc: He says many a beautiful thing of you, such that I might suspect he has mastered his tongue long ago. Where's Sailing Master? He likes to pop in randomly.

Jules: A mastered tongue knows when it should be used and when it should be still. Who the hell cares where Luther is? Probably off fishing with the Lagoon Maiden crew.

Doc: You are more impatient than a seagull with its sights set on your lunch.

Jules: Spill it, Doc.

Doc: Can you ditch this evening to go carousing? Roman will meet up with you. Oh, and he left you a bag. Said it was a present.
(gives bag)

Jules: (takes out rope ladder) A ladder? What is this, a pre-wedding party? I'm not exactly intere—You're giving me that look you gave me when you said I didn't have a choice in keeping my eye. Don't let me get myself in trouble.

Exeunt Jules and Doc

SCENE 6

ACT 2, SCENE 6

NORTH DOCKS:
The Red Lantern

Enter Roman and Madam Linley

Madam Linley: May Hymenaeus smile down on you for this.

Roman: I have left candles at the shrines asking for blessings to see us step from under the shadow of our captains' flags and into our own.

Madam Linley: Remember to reef your sails when the wind blows too hard, lest your ship crashes against the breakers. Love is not a calm day on a windless sea. It is waking up and absorbing yourself in the swell in the waves. It's holding on tight when the storm lashes. It's crawling into a warm berth when ice coats the decks. It's learning when to change course. Listen to the creak in the mast. Watch for leaks. Patch. Mend. Paint. It's sitting and letting the current talk to you when nothing else makes sense. It won't

break apart under hurricane or typhoon as
long as you take care of it.

Enter Jules

Madam Linley: The same goes for you to know
of love. To know that it is not a force to work
against, but to work with. It is a matter of
taking the hand offered you and letting it
pull you along when you grow weary, and
tugging on it when it tires. It is knowing that
you are not setting out to change the person,
instead setting out to grow with them, and
they you. It is not an easy course. Four letters
make the word. Simple to whisper in dark
corners and as pet names. It is a heavy
weight and a feather-light embrace. No
simpler than the rotation of the stars in the
skies and the cycles of the tides. One minute
you will drown in it, another you will fly
with it.

Jules: Nice to visit with you again, Madam. It's
been too long.

Madam Linley: Well over a year, it has. Thought
I'd give Roman a taste of his own medicine
for the number of nights he's spent asking us
our thoughts on love, the universe, the stars'
passage, and the morning tide.

Jules: It is sweet for a medicine.

Roman: You're not mad at me for visiting a place
like this?

Jules: You found us a captain, didn't you? How
can I be angry for you holding up your side

of the bargain? And Madam's lilies have always been gracious when I've found my evening here.

Madam Linley: And both of you talk on as reincarnation of Thoth, walking through our halls, rather than the gardeners who occupy our hedges. We thought for a time that you had died and reincarnated to bless us with Roman. It will save all our sanity that you found each other. Now, about that ceremony. You both brought your contracts, right?

Exeunt all

ACT 3

SCENE 1

SQUANDERER'S BAY: THE MARKET

Enter Malone, Bostock, Gunner and Crimson Blade Crew

Bostock: The heat makes everyone stupid. Malone, let's go back to the ship. People are just edging for a crossed blade, and I would rather not be a cross Blade. The Albatrosses are already eyeing us, ready to pick us off.

Malone: Water from the gods, a thimble full alone, will bring you to crossing Blades with Albatrosses. Regardless of the weather.

Bostock: Oh, Lord, no one's ever told me I'm a fighting drunk.

Malone: Drunk or otherwise, you toe the line of your razor's edge more than most when there's something for you to be angry about.

Bostock: Get to the point before I do.

Malone: If there were two of you, there would be none of you. To find someone else to compete with you is none other than your ever-persistent desire in life.

Bostock: You think I fight so much, I would

never see the end of the medical bills if I fought like you.

Malone: Then learn not to get hurt.

Enter Tyndall, Boatswain, and Black Albatross Crew

Bostock: Lutterell's men are here.

Malone: I'm gonna pretend I didn't hear that. I've no business with them.

Tyndall: (to Boatswain and Crew) Close now, guys. I need to have a chat with them.

(to Crimson Blade Crew) Mind if I have a word?

Malone: You can have a word. However, I might suggest taking more than just the one word. Makes for better conversation.

Tyndall: I would if you'd shut up.

Malone: Rude much.

Tyndall: Malone, you're part of the Blade. You know Roman, right? Hang around him, aye?

Malone: Is there a point to your question closer than the tip of the blade at your hip?

Bostock: Easy, man. You're being grouchy, and we don't want a bloodbath in the street. Take it elsewhere if you can't keep a civil tongue in your head.

Malone: Tell that to the Albatross. They've never kept a civil tongue with us, and you know it. If old Tin-Tin's showed up, you know they're just itching to find the depth of our guts.

Enter Roman

Tyndall: Fortuna presents me with my requests.

Malone: He is no present, yours' or others'.

Tyndall: Roman. All I can say is you're a
right cad.

Roman: I have no fault with you, Tyndall. Less
so now than ever. Clearly, I'm not wanted
here, though, so I'm just gonna go.

Tyndall: Neither wanted here nor Jones's locker.
You have put me in a place I don't like being.
Now I shall have it righted. Turn and draw!

Roman: I have no reason to have any qualm
between you and me. You may not know it
yet, but neither do you.

Malone: Roman, where has your spine gone?
(draws sword) The Grim Reaper is wanting a
soul. Fine, I'll give him a bit of an ego stroke.

Tyndall: I don't need you to stroke my ego.

Malone: You need to go stroke something if
you're here trying to duel Roman over who
knows what malarky you and The Black
Albatross crew have invented for yourselves
today. The man is gentle as a dove and
averse to pissing someone off. So, who's
gone and pissed all over your bread
pudding? I'd bet you a madam kicked you
from a berth earlier than you planned, and
now you're just hot under the collar trying to
blow steam, seeing as you couldn't blow it
earlier.

Tyndall: A sword to the tongue will stop your
infernal yammering. (draws sword)

Roman: Oye, oye, oye, mate. Malone, put it
away. It's hot and miserable out, and you

aren't thinking straight. Come on. Let's go grab something to eat. You aren't yourself when you're hungry. Ice cream? How does that sound?

Malone: It's not the heat. He's been dying to taste steel every time he's come near us for no reason at all. Even now, he is pressing you to a duel.

Malone and Tyndall Fight

Roman: Oh, damn it all! Bostock, help me with these idiots. Gov's gonna be on us like fleas on dogs at this rate, and you know I puke if I see blood. Malone, cut it out!

Roman struggles to break up the fight. Tyndall stabs Malone.

Boatswain: Let's get out of here, Tyndall. This is going to get bad.

Exeunt The Black Albatross Crew

Malone: Skewered like a stuck pig, I've been. May Hades damn both the crews.

Bostock: Malone! Malone! You're bleeding. We need to get it to stop. Shut up and sit still before you take tea and biscuits in Davy Jones's parlour for real.

Malone: Oh, that hurts a lot more than I'd like to admit. And I've admitted a lot in my short lifetime. Cabin boy! Grab a medic, would you?

Exit cabin boy

Roman: Blood flows from your wounds like words tumble from your lips, and one of those fonts needs be stifled. As yet I am wanting for a way to staunch the more pressing one, so I beg of you: shut your yap for a bit until the doc gets here.

Malone: It doesn't look that bad. Feels bad. Doesn't....well, no, that does actually look pretty bad. Think a doc can patch that? Why'd you get in the way? I couldn't deflect him with you blocking my view. Jeez, ow, ow, ow, ow, ow. May both the ships sink for this.

Roman: Sorry, sorry, sorry. I was trying to get you to quit and didn't want Tyndall getting you hurt, and I'm so sorry, Malone.

Malone: Bostock, I see flies already coming our way in this heat. Can you get me somewhere cool and maybe less likely to end up with maggots in my wounds until I pass across death's door?

Exeunt Malone and Bostock

Roman: Oh crap, oh shit, oh crap. No, no, no, no, no. This is bad. This is really bad. I go and get married, and neither Jules nor I have qualms with the Albatross or the Blade now, and Tyndall doesn't even know he doesn't need to see us as enemies anymore, and then this goes down. This isn't good.

Enter Bostock

Bostock: It doesn't look good, Roman. The medic told me to get out of the way. I don't—I don't know what to say.

Roman: I don't think there is anything to say. Malone's not wrong. Both the crews have been fighting so much. This was inevitable. If only the Blade and the Albatross could keep a real truce. See the good side in each other. Friendly competition four decades ago that turned into this—this—this mess. We both serve the same crown, and yet we cannot privateer in peace.

Enter Tyndall followed shortly after by the Market Watch

Bostock: Haven't you done enough, Tyndall?

Roman: You bloody well probably killed him, Tyndall! You come here calling me some kind of a cad while you yourself plunge blade into flesh. Have I yet laid hand to you or drawn sword in want of shield? I had no qualm against you or yours, but you have right given me reason to turn into your reprobate. Pray, give me damn good reason not to.

Tyndall: You are as much a rogue as ever there were. I need not give you reason. You existing is reason enough. Leave me and mine alone. Take Malone's passing as warning to steer clear of The Black Albatross. (Attacks with sword)

Roman: (Lunges with drawn blade, sinking into Tyndall's heart) He's not dead yet, but you will be greeting Davy Jones soon for that. You wanted a villain; take my face with you to the next world and know me a monster. There are reasons I don't draw a blade.

Bostock: Quick, Roman, get out of here. The Market Watch is here, and soon too will the Gov. He won't be kind to you or the Blade for outright murder.

Roman: I claim this as self-defence, and no one of the Watch will say otherwise. (looking to those in the Market Watch, who nod) The difference between privateer and pirate. Looks like I've finally crossed that line, Bostock. And it is a line between you and me. I will return to check on Malone. Leave this letter with Captain Montgomery. I meant to give it to her this morning. (Hands Bostock letter)

Bostock: Through thick and thin, a line no thinner than a nib scratch or wider than the log lines on a map can part us long, my friend. I shall deliver this and then be close behind. Madam Linley has told me of a voyage with a new treasure you are to quartermaster, and I am keen to jump ship and run with you. Now go.

Exit Roman

First Market Watch: Let's get this straight. I saw nothing. Tyndall attacked you, Roman,

and Malone out of the blue for no good
reason, yes?

Bostock: Yes.

First Market Watch: Malone got himself skewered by Tyndall, roundly fought him off.
Tyndall died, and Malone is in hospital and
Roman got scared off while you returned
from taking Malone to get treated. Got it?

*Enter Governor, Captain Lutterell, Sailing Master Luther, Captain
Montgomery, and others*

Governor: Neighbourhood watch, explain this
mess on my streets.

Bostock: Gov, it was all some kind of misunderstanding. Malone and I were out fetching
supplies for the ship, and Tyndall came
demanding Roman for some reason.

Sailing Master Luther: The black-hearted
scourge of a quartermaster should have
never left his decks! Tyndall does not
deserve to be lying here in the gutter.

Governor: Peace, Luther. We must determine
what has happened before laying blame
where it needn't fester. Bostock, why is there
a dead man at my feet?

Bostock: Honest, true to Veritas's ears, might
she curse me into an early grave, I tell you,
Malone did nothing but defend against a
warrantless attack. I took him to an infirmary with grave injuries, only to return
here and find Tyndall having passed from
his wounds. I could not carry both. I am

sorry, Sailing Master Luther, Governor, Captains.

Sailing Master Luther: Veritas's ears be damned, you lying dog. Tyndall would never do something so untoward as to ambush someone in broad daylight.

Governor: Shut it, Luther. I have appeased that man myself more than once from seeking justice upon lesser souls. This is now the fifth time I've been called on you pirates. Send word to your bondsman with the Privateers' Office. Both the Blade and Albatross are hereby exiled from Squanderer's Bay. You have a fortnight to replenish stock and see that your ships never dock here again. Those who wish to cancel their contracts with Albatross or Blade and not be labelled a pirate may come to my office, and I will release their names. You are all now considered pirates within these bays and harbours. All who keep to your ships will be marked as pirate in the registry. Any pirate stepping foot in Squanderer's Bay and is known as such shall be put to the hangman's grasp.

Captain Montgomery: Please don't set Roman or Bostock as a pirate in this, Governor. They had nothing to do with a battle between Malone or Tyndall. They have always broken up fights or been absent from them.

Governor: That much, I have seen in truth. I will consider the words of a pirate this once, Captain Montgomery. They will be granted

leniency and marked as such. Neither you
nor Lutterell could control your crews. Now I
will control them for you. Leave. You have a
fortnight. After that, if your ship is docked,
your men are here, or your warehouses full,
all will be commandeered by the Governance
of Squanderer's Bay and thereby become
property of the state. A man is dead on my
streets, and one lies dying in an infirmary
because of your rash actions and leniency.
I say no more. You have broken the truce and
your promise too many times.
The next I see you, there will be gallows waiting.

Exeunt all

SCENE 2

SQUANDERER'S BAY: CAPTAIN LUTTERALL'S WAREHOUSE

Enter Jules

> **Jules:** Can the night not come sooner? I would wish a darkness where blessed fingers found hidden pleasures. One last night in these cabins. Soon, I shall join my Roman on my new ship, and we will find the edge of the horizon together.

Enter Doc with rope ladder

> **Jules:** You look worried, Doc. What's up?
> **Doc:** Tyndall's dead. He attacked Malone from The Crimson Blade in broad daylight. He was after Roman.
> **Jules:** He's dead? That's not...that can't be right. Tyndall's the best swordsman around. He's the Grim Reaper, the Scythe of The Black Albatross. Are you sure it isn't another?
> **Doc:** It's Tyndall all right. Hot-headed and now cold-blooded.

Jules: But why? Why go after Roman?

Doc: He thought Roman was spying on The Black Albatross when he turned up as Hamlet at the party. Tyndall went to confront him and got himself stabbed through the heart for his efforts.

Jules: Are you sure it was Malone who did it?

Doc: I'd wager not. Malone could roughhouse like the rest of them, but he wasn't raised a Verne. The house's sword technique is all over that injury Tyndall took.

Jules: Verne. As in Roman Verne? You think Roman killed him?

Doc: I'd wager every pearl in the hold that Roman did it.

Jules: Roman can't stand blood. Everyone knows that. He's practically a pacifist. The Crimson Blade isn't known for this.

Doc: You aren't wrong. You aren't right either. He was why the ship was named The Crimson Blade. Montgomery ran a different ship before meeting him. Roman can't stand blood because oath under the Verne name said that a blade drawn cannot be returned to the scabbard unless a heart stops beating upon it. He holds that oath to this day. He doesn't pull it unless he knows he's killing somebody.

Jules: Tyndall's dead. Roman killed him. Where does that leave us?

Doc: You still taking Roman to bed with you?

Jules: Not like I haven't killed a man in battle

before. I'm not about to hold it against him for defending himself against Tyndall. You and I both know we had no love for the man. Why do you look like you drank poison?

Doc: We're all being exiled from the Bay. Governor has issued a decree that The Black Albatross and The Crimson Blade shall be listed as pirate ships and no longer welcomed here. Crew are being offered the opportunity to cancel their privateer contracts with Montgomery and Lutterell at the Governor's office so they are not labelled as pirate in the logbooks.

Jules: Where will this leave you?

Doc: I don't know, Jules. I don't know. I've been with Lutterell for too many years to count now. I wouldn't know what to make of an infirmary that did not rock beneath my feet. As it is, Bostock and Roman have been already provided leniency from the pirate label. Governor took the Market Watch's word that Malone and Tyndall fought, not Roman, and that it was Malone's blade that found Tyndall's heart. So, as for crown and country, Roman is not a pirate.

Jules: Are you willing to break contract with Lutterell?

Doc: Yes? What are you up to, Jules?

Jules: Take your contract to the governor, then meet me at The Red Lantern.

Doc: Jules?

Jules: Just do it. I think I just found a good use

for that ladder Roman left with me. (Takes ladder)

Exeunt Jules and Doc

SCENE 3

Madam Linley enters

Madam Linley: You blasted Verne. You seriously couldn't leave your blade sheathed? Now the whole docks are in an uproar with both your crew and Jules' crew getting the boot.

Roman enters

Roman: No, they aren't. My crew, until they are planted in the paradise you never stop talking about, is still taking on patrons as far as I've seen. Now, my prior crew, yes, they are in shambles. I will never apologise for being a Verne or sharing that name with my Jules.

Madam Linley: The Governor has condemned both The Crimson Blade and The Black Albatross. They are marked as pirates as of today! You don't think this is a problem?

Roman: Not as far as I'm concerned. They

fought non-stop, no matter what Bostock or
I or even Lutterell's physician did. Do you
think I wanted to be bound to a contract
with people who couldn't even control their
own impulses?

Madam Linley: Says the guy I just helped get
married and become the quartermaster of
The Red Lantern on a whim.

Roman: You saw opportunity for yourself just as
much as I did. Do not blame my impulses if
you do not account for your own.

Madam Linley: Save it, blackguard. You didn't
need to kill the man, and you know it. You
could have maimed him at the very least and
left him alive.

Roman: You would have me look into the eyes of
a killer calling me a villain, who has already
put a hole in my friend, and take a knife to
the gut? You would have me die on the blade
of a man hell-bent on an unnamed
vengeance he did not wish to discuss? I
played the saint. I appeased. I tried. If I had
not ended things the way I did, I would be
bleeding out on the streets of Squanderer's
Bay, and you would be without a navigator.
You would rather I not get you to paradise,
Madam Linley? You have yet to set foot on
this paradise you talk of. You turned over the
fortune of The Red Lantern to Jules and me
as new captain and quartermaster in
exchange that you would have a place to set
permanent foot, and you would accuse me of
impulsively defending myself? A single

thrust to the heart was merciful compared to
what I have seen others of the privateers do
to men.

You've seen them, Madam. The tongue-less, the
whipped, the tortured. If I wished for moral-
ity, I would have taken up the cloak and laid
down my blade long ago. You would think
me some gentle soul like the rest of them. I
am a pirate. I crossed that line long ago, my
Lady. I am damned to the depths of Davy
Jones's locker where I will meet Tyndall
again one day. I face that fate knowing it,
and you would condemn me here and now?

Call me a blackguard, Madam, and I will know
you have no good intentions for me or mine.

Madam Linley: Calm yourself, Roman.

Roman: You think this is easy, Madam? I haven't
set a blade in a heart in decades, not since
my voice scaled heaven's ladder. The time I
did left me stranded on a desert island with
no food and a half-empty flask of water. No
goodwill came from that man's intentions
revolving around me. It was only my own
damn fault for discovering him to be the
Sailing Master for The Murderous Ghost
after protecting myself, and a blessing the
captain did not kill me there and then. I do
not pluck petals from community gardens
for reasons, Madam Linley. The Murderous
Ghost's Sailing Master is one.

Madam Linley: Murderous Ghost? As in the
largest sailing brothel ship on the seas? You
were a lily? I thought you were a rose!

Roman: Not a lily. Murderous Ghost doesn't hire as you do. They kidnap. They thought me one of their acquisitions. The Sailing Master decided to try something, and I buried my blade to the hilt in his chest for his attempts.

Madam Linley: Oh, Roman, I didn't know. I'm so sorry.

Roman: There's nothing to be sorry for. Just don't call me a blackguard, or a villain, or a cad, or a rogue for protecting myself. I've had enough of being called names today. I am putting you and yours on a paradise island, and then going on a hunt for a flock of murderous ghosts and maybe, for once in years, look for my family. See if any of them survived the pillaging when the Ghosts came through our city. I keep my sword sheathed for reasons, Madam. Don't think I will pull it here without thought.

Madam Linley: Who do you pray to at night, Roman?

Roman: Any god willing to listen. No god when I know what I ask is unreasonable.

Madam Linley: Then will you promise to Aphrodite that you will not wield a sword on this ship?

Roman: No.

Madam Linley: Why?

Roman: It becomes impractical for me to be weaponless when someone boards this vessel wanting to take advantage of my crew. You are part of my crew now, and I will protect you and all the lilies on it. If you take

my sword, you take out of your garden the
thorn protecting your flowers from being
plucked by ghostly fingers.

Madam Linley: Then I will allow a wild thorn to
grow in my garden if only to ward off the
ephemeral.

Enter Doc

Doc: It has turned into complete chaos out
there. Governor didn't realise how important the crews were to Squanderer's Bay.
Others of the privateers are weighing
anchor as we speak. Shop stalls are closing
up. He didn't know just how many were
being run by crews. This is going to get
really bad. Jules sent me with a voided
contract from the Governor's office. What is
this all about?

Madam Linley: A voided contract? You aren't
part of The Black Albatross anymore?

Doc: Not anymore. Do you know why they
would send me here?

Madam Linley: Jules is captain of The Red
Lantern as of last night. If they sent you here
with a voided contract, they're probably
hoping to sign you onto their crew once they
arrive.

Doc: They're captain?

Roman: I'd rather they be captain. I can navigate all day and night, but they're known for
taking their captain's place more often than
not. They have the experience for it.

Doc: That was not what I expected, especially
   coming from a Verne.

Roman: Watch it, Doc.

Doc: I thought you were supposed to be some
   floral-languaged calf crying to the moon
   about love. You really are just a bloodthirsty
   pirate.

Roman: I don't have to cross-sign that contract
   if I don't want to, Doc. You're toeing a line I
   will give you one warning about.

Madam Linley: We can be civil here, gentlemen.
   Now is not a time to dredge old history. For
   the time being, let's get Doc settled in until
   Jules shows up and we can be done with this
   whole fiasco.

Doc: I do not want to be a member of a crew for
   a villain.

Roman: Oh, sweet Guanyin, please deliver me
   from this horrible day. I just wanted to enjoy
   my honeymoon and be about my life. I am
   not a villain. Of all things, why am I the one
   over here being called names? All I did was
   find someone I fell in love with and got
   married. What is so wrong with finding
   love?

Doc: You were spying on The Black Albatross
   when you came to Prodigal Son dressed as
   Hamlet.

Roman: For the love of Koalemos! Bostock and
   Malone took me along because I was
   suffering from heartbreak and they thought
   a bit of some fun would put me in a chipper

mood. We weren't there to do anything wrong by it.

Madam Linley: You see, Doc? Roman is just a sap who's decent with a sword.

Roman: I prefer waxing lyrical over dusting a blade. What a mess.

Exeunt all

SCENE 4

NORTH DOCKS:
CABIN IN
The Black Albatross

Enter Captain Lutterell, Sailing Master Luther, and Captain Parker

Captain Lutterell: I'm not entirely sure how everything has suddenly turned altogether wrong. I'm going to have to give up my crew at this rate. Lawrence from the Privateer's Office has been after me for ten years to take my retirement. Now, like a djinn from its lamp, the master might get his wish. The old fart.

Look, Captain Parker, I don't want Jules caught up in all of this. Are you still keen on having them as a quartermaster? I would think shifting them over to the Naval Office wouldn't be too difficult. Might need Gov to write a letter of recommendation or something. Jules has never been near any of these squabbles between the Blade and us. I really don't see it being a problem.

Captain Parker: Reason why I'm here, sir. I received a note from the Governor explaining what is going on and that you were looking into closing up shop. Word had it that you were even going to sell the ship? That feels rather drastic. What about you, Luther? Would you take the ship and be the new captain? Maybe a change of hand at the helm would yield a new bounty to the hold. Though, the potential of a quartermaster...?

Sailing Master Luther: You still wish Jules to be your quartermaster, I'm aware, Parker. They have taken to their bunk this evening, for once away from the infirmary bay, and I do not wish to upset Doc in disturbing his charge's sleep. They will not have many an evening left to enjoy it, sad to say.

To return, though, to the ship's providence, I believe it the mark of the fool to rename a ship. A curse I would not wish upon any man. No, I will not take up the helm and call myself captain of The Black Albatross. It has been registered a pirate ship, after all.

Captain Lutterell: A needless notion, Luther. No ill has begotten a ship in these harbours yet that has received a new name. If you do not wish to captain though, my old friend, I will not force you. It is an arduous task as it is. See the folios gathered upon my desk gathering dust with the lack of time I have to see them. If you will not take up the helm, I shall need to sell it. Jules will have to leave the ship. This I guarantee, if I am to sell it. Then, what will become of my quartermaster? They will become free to find a new perch, and a new career with you would be the most advantageous of all. The shipman's auction runs on Wednesdays. Wait. What's today?

Captain Parker: Monday, as far as I know.

Captain Lutterell: A passing on a Monday is never a good omen. Death at any time is not. To lose Tyndall on a Monday. Let me think. We have a fortnight's time to evict the crew and move the ship from the Bay or sell it. I would think, after Tyndall's funeral…Would Thursday work for you to meet at the Naval Office for Jules's contract transfer? That doesn't sound unreasonable to me. Let's.

Captain Parker: Then I will anticipate a transference and meet Jules at the Naval Office on Thursday.

Captain Lutterell: Luther, see to it that Jules is ready to transfer ships and papers. I wish that I could retain them as quartermaster, but there is no saving this mess. They were one of the best I've had. They'll be stationed with the Naval Office if I have to twist Gov's arm. (to Captain Parker) Good day to you, sir. I hope we meet on better terms when next we see each other.

Exeunt all

SCENE 5

SQUANDERER'S BAY: CAPTAIN LUTTERALL'S WAREHOUSE

Enter Roman and Jules on the roof of the warehouse

Jules: All you can hear are the waves. The gulls are silent yet. Late enough still that no one will be here. No one save us. Quite a bit of the crew has already evicted themselves like rats on a sinking ship.

Roman: You say that, and yet the pink of the sun is pulling itself over the edge of rooftops like a dying man in sight of water. Are you certain the warehouse has not been emptied yet?

Jules: I've been perched up here most of yesterday, and no one has made time to visit. It's not crew pay or storage, so no one other than Captain, Luther, and I have reason to be here.

Roman: Your perch should not be in a cage. I would not have a net strangle your pretty plumage for a shiny rock.

Jules: A nest in the winds at the edge of the

horizon awaits us. A shiny rock is all we need to make it possible. Like a raven, I took a liking to its sparkle. I can split with its faceted edge if it means we fly free.

Roman: Then it is time to cleave it from its aggregate. I only hope to climb into this mine shaft and not encounter a beast interested in eating me.

Enter Doc on warehouse roof

Doc: First you put a hole in Tyndall, and now we're on the roof of Lutterell's warehouse. Are you trying to get hung for piracy?

Jules: We're only pirates if we get caught, and it's for my provisions anyways. I just don't have the key to get in and would rather not have the "I'm leaving" conversation with Captain right now.

Doc: And you made me a part of this conspiracy.

Jules: (to Roman) You ready?

Roman: Mahogany jewelry box, hand-sized, south end of the warehouse near a large mirror. Can't miss it. Gold lock.

Jules: It's gonna be heavy. Make sure it's secure before you try to climb the rope back up.

Roman: Will you be this much of a worry when we're off on our first voyage together?

Jules: And our fiftieth.

Roman: Then I think I found a good captain for us.

Jules: I hear footsteps; fly, my love.

Roman: Like the pigeon, I will find my way
　　home again.

Jules: I will watch the clouds for your return.

Exit Roman down the ladder; Jules and Doc leave the roof a different
way
Enter Sailing Master Luther on street level

Sailing Master Luther: Jules! Jules Road, where
　　have you gotten yourself off to?

Enter Jules on street level

Jules: Luther? What are you doing awake at this
　　time of day?

Sailing Master Luther: Contemplating the
　　ending of our days. Bidding many a long and
　　sad goodbye to what has been our second
　　home. And you, Quartermaster? What is
　　dawn's light telling you of the passage of
　　time?

Jules: Time to me is only a suggestion. And with
　　its passage, I have learned that I have the
　　edge of the world to look forward to.

Sailing Master Luther: I fear that I no longer
　　have the waves to look to. With Lutterell's
　　retirement, so shall I retire. You have yet to
　　wear your age like a weathered cloak. One
　　day though.

Jules: Where will you hang your cloak if you will
　　not walk the rolling deck, Sailing Master?

Sailing Master Luther: I foresee a chair on a

porch. One overlooking the sunset on a beach. Maybe where pearls lay in the blue.

Jules: Then you will not be so far from your beloved waves, Luther. You will only obtain a new perspective: one that brings you the rewards, rather than you chasing after.

Sailing Master Luther: A fickle mistress, the waves have always been by my side and yet so unattainable. What would it be to stand in the rivulets in a summer breeze?

Jules: I believe in a different kind of peace, one well earned.

Sailing Master Luther: One found before the bottom of a grave. Would you call that a different kind of peace?

Jules: We all mourn Tyndall's death in our own way. In a fashion, we are mourning the loss of our family, under threat of the Governor. May they both find peace in their own decisions.

Sailing Master Luther: You and Tyndall never quite got along. You do not mourn like some.

Jules: And yet I have laid the first flowers on his grave in a bid to part on better terms than we lived. What is mourning if not reconciliation with the threads the Fates chose to cut? Eventually, you must knot the ends before they become the entire tapestry's undoing.

Sailing Master Luther: You have heard who it was that forced him to participate in an early meeting with Lord Hades?

Jules: Malone, from the reports I heard.

Sailing Master Luther: I have word that it may have been Roman.

Jules: That man? He fears the edge of a blade, the blood pooling. He ran away before Tyndall's blade even found the road. No, don't think anything of it. He is not to be faulted for Tyndall's recklessness.

Sailing Master Luther: You don't think Roman did it?

Jules: I believe that I am no investigator, grave digger, priest, or medium by which to provide a clear answer. Bostock was the only one there that saw what happened. I will trust him at his word and wish for peace between what was The Crimson Blade and The Black Albatross.

Sailing Master Luther: You would trust a Blade so simply?

Jules: I trust in Tyndall's animosity and Roman's search for equilibrium.

Sailing Master Luther: Would you trust your own feelings?

Enter Captain Lutterell

Captain Lutterell: Ah, Jules, Luther, just who I was looking for. Have you told Jules about Captain Parker?

Sailing Master Luther: No, not as of yet, sir. We were discussing Tyndall; may he rest in peace.

Captain Lutterell: May he find his new path through the wheels of heaven. (To Jules)

Captain Parker is insisting that you join with the crown and become his new quartermaster. I would see that you were well cared for, and this is an opportunity that would set your career path forward cleanly. As an old man's few remaining gifts, can I see you established in safety?

Jules: I would wish to thank you for a generous gift, one given to see to my betterment.

Captain Lutterell: Would wish? Is this not a fine gift? One that will take you beyond even my means? Take you on a path that would see you finding a life appreciated by the citizenship? One where you could walk the city streets and not need to hide who you are?

Sailing Master Luther: This is an opportunity you otherwise will not have, Jules. Please, don't throw this away. A position with Parker is something us privateers just can't get any day.

Jules: If I could have a word?

Captain Lutterell: You use so many words. I have given you all that I had. You've taken them and thrown them in my face just as much as you've squandered them on your whimsical fantasies.

Enter Doc

Doc: Why are you yelling at Jules when you haven't given them space enough to catch their breath?

Captain Lutterell: Shut it, doc! I was wrong to

worry so much. They throw my gift in my face. Unwilling. Wretched scoundrel whose only desire is to advance themself beyond their means. I should have never stuck my neck out for them. Now I risk a noose cinching around it.

Doc: Sir, you will put yourself to bed if you continue to let your anger take the best of you.

Captain Lutterell: You would side with this swindling thief? A true pirate to not take a commission to the crown!

Doc: Now you lay words in my mouth, like a mother's spoon to a weaning babe who wishes nothing more than milk from the source.

Captain Lutterell: You are no captain, or child. You are no ship's steward. What do you know of the sea, doctor? Nothing. You specialise in keeping a man's heart beating, but you know nothing of keeping a man from sinking. This is not your conversation to be in.

Sailing Master Luther: Captain, your heart!

Captain Lutterell: My heart, my heart. I laid my heart out on the line to see to that useless quartermaster's life being easy and yet here I am surrounded by people angry at me for making an effort. No. No. I will not have it. (to Jules) Never show your face in front of me ag—oh my chest. I—I think I'm done here.

Jules: Captain! Luther, see to him. He doesn't look well.

Sailing Master Luther: Aye, Jules. I'll see to him.

Exeunt Captain Lutterell and Sailing Master Luther

Jules: What was that about? I left notice with Lutterell that I would be withdrawing my contract yesterday. Now he's got it in his head that I'll be a quartermaster to Parker? To the Crown? I'd rather hang from the mainmast than be that man's quartermaster.

Doc: Did you hand him the paper?

Jules: He wasn't in his office when I dropped by. I left it on top of his working pile. Label and everything, that he'd see it when he sat back down.

Doc: If you didn't hand it to him, he probably didn't read it. Honestly, Jules, I wouldn't worry too much about it. You and I both know that he has been on the shortlist for retirement for quite a few years now. How often did you take over as captain in place of him before your incident?

Jules: You would think, with Luther so close at his heels, Captain would press to have him be acting captain more than me.

Doc: What of Roman? Will you return to him? Will he run with your treasure?

Jules: Where would he run that I would not find him, Doc? Why would I not return to him or he to me? He is my quartermaster. I am his captain. We have been joined by knot and by

contract. This mess between the Albatross
and the Blade? I am already away and
finding the edge of my horizon.

Doc: You have no feelings for the crew? The
family that took you in when you had nothing? I thought you would be at a loss.
Indeed, you may just be more pirate than
Tyndall. You give me no sign of remorse.
Then I will return to The Red Lantern and
wait for you there. Send Palmer if you find a
need for me.

Jules: It is not that I am without despondency
for the crew. It is that I am choosing my
family now, rather than having it chosen
for me.

Exeunt all

ACT 4

SCENE 1

NORTH DOCKS: CAPTAIN'S CABIN

The Red Lantern

Madam Linley: You would evict all the brothel ships from Scoundrel's Bay? Does his Majesty wish for the privateers dismantled in their entirety? We leave, this place will snap like an angry clam.

Captain Parker: His Majesty has long wished for this black market to sink below the waves. That it took this long has been surprising.

Madam Linley: Did you have something to do with Tyndall from The Black Albatross?

Captain Parker: It is not that I had something to do necessarily. A letter from Roman crossed my fingers and made its way to Tyndall is all.

Madam Linley: A false Rome will never best a real Ceasar.

Captain Parker: I do not see him playing a fiddle, but a match sparks a conflagration, and there are beautiful hills beyond the limits from which the fire will be magnificent to watch.

Enter Jules

Jules: Parker. What are you doing here?

Captain Parker: My quartermaster! Perfect timing. I've been meaning for a chat, just you and me, to discuss your joining with His Majesty's Navy. I trust that Captain Lutterell has mentioned it?

Jules: Captain Lutterell has, though as it stands currently, could you refrain from calling me your anything? I've signed no contract with His Majesty's Navy as of yet.

Captain Parker: It won't be long, though, until that signature blossoms across the contract like a finely trimmed hydrangea.

Madam Linley: It does bloom finely when applied.

Captain Parker: I may wish to see a hydrangea blossom, but it looks to me that you've come for a lily's bud.

Jules: If I were to answer that, would it make you a lily in the Crown's hand?

Captain Parker: Only so far as the cheque reaches.

Jules: It seems to reach quite far.

Captain Parker: If you saw the size of it, I think you'd be happy with the circumstances too.

Jules: I'm good with the depths I accept already. It doesn't chaff.

Captain Parker: I think this conversation has escaped me.

Jules: If only it were the only thing to escape

your notice. What of the contracts? Have they escaped you?

Captain Parker: I've read them close enough, letters a plethora upon the page, a purse of dandelion seeds upended with so much fluff.

Jules: Enough to see the burs hidden amongst the pappus? Or are hydrangea petals all you see?

Captain Parker: Whether a field of hydrangeas or a field of dandelions, your petals belong to me.

Jules: I still belong to my own contract, sir. And I'd prefer not find myself planted in with so many weeds. As that stands, I make my lofty escape, like a dandelion seed upon the breeze. Madam Linley, is there an open berth below?

Madam Linley: I'll show you where you can plant yourself for the evening, my finely petaled friend. Parker, it was nice talking.

Captain Parker: I wouldn't dream of getting in the way of someone's enjoyable evening. It frustrates me as it is when someone comes knocking, and I have better things to do. So, I bid adieu, and remind you to speak with your captain. I will have your contract for the Crown in hand by the end of the week.

Exit Captain Parker

Jules: Madam, if I ever sign a contract with that man, promise to shoot me with that broad cannon of yours.

Madam Linley: I would surely miss our lovely discussions, but I would not blame you such a desire. It sounds to me that he is determined to gain it, though. I have heard ill word of his methods. He set up Roman. He did. I would swear it upon Aphrodite's mantle. He will come for you. Be prepared for his amorous perusal to strangle. Do not trust him.

Jules: I am my own captain and yet I must yet berth as a quartermaster, Madam, while all the players on the board are in motion. The wait to weigh anchor is like watching the clock for sign of movement when the key has been forgotten. I have held between my fingers my life choices. A new name. A new fate. A new garden upon these decks by which to blossom. It is but a few days before I can take the helm in my fingers and dance along its surface, turning the wave beneath my keel. And yet that infernal creature comes snooping around making needless demands, taking away my sunshine in a moment of happiness. He's persistent. If he is as you say, and under commission to the crown, he is liable towards untoward methods.

Madam Linley: More so than others I have seen walk these boards. He would squander away your fine dowry if he were to detain Roman. I say then, let's outrun him.

Jules: He captains the fastest brigantine in the Crown's fleet, Madam.

Madam Linley: And I gave you the fastest ship in Squanderer's Bay. A fourth rated with full riggings against a brigantine rigged to the code?

Jules: Is it faster than the Crown?

Madam Linley: The Crown docks its fleet in Squanderer's Bay, does it not?

Jules: Then I shall unfurl the sails and let the wind take us where it will. Be ready. Have the lilies prepare their spring showing and bid farewell to their lovely gardeners. I will take us from this dried-up soil and have you to paradise before Captain Parker can wade through all the many contracts sprawled across the Governor's desk.

E*xeunt Jules and Madam Linley*

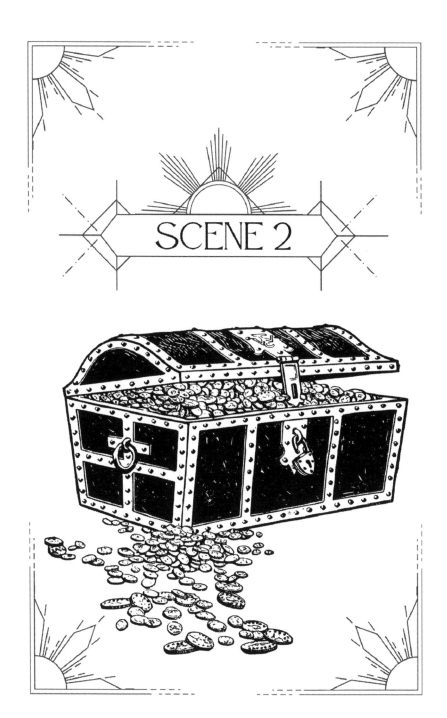

SCENE 2

ACT 4, SCENE 2

NORTH DOCKS: HALL IN
The Black Albatross

Enter Captain Lutterell with Sailing Master Luther, Doc, and two to three Galley Help

> **Captain Lutterell:** (giving the First Galley Help a sheet of paper) See that all of The Black Albatross are here, everyone on this list, along with those of Captain Parker's crew.
>
> *Exit the First Galley Help*
>
> (to Second Galley Help) Go find Cook some extra help. There will not be nearly enough hands on deck for this feast.
>
> **Second Galley Help:** I'll find you the best I can, sir.
>
> **Captain Lutterell:** As long as they refrain from poisoning us, I'll take it.
>
> *Exit the Second Galley Help*
>
> I am not ready to give up this ship, or the best quartermaster that has ever served under me, but such are the times.
>
> (to Doc) What? Has my quartermaster gone off to seek comfort in a lily bed?

Doc: They have gone to speak with Madam
Linley.

Captain Lutterell: Maybe Jules'll come back a
bit more levelled off for it. They've gained a
bit of hard-headed contradiction since
losing their eye.

Enter Jules

Doc: From that expression, I'd say they reached
well beyond levelled off and found ecstasy.

Captain Lutterell: And how is my hard-headed
quartermaster of late? Where have you been?
Sightseeing the Crown's Navy?

Jules: I have seen much of the Crown's Navy in
the last few days, Captain. Their ships gleam
as if never having fought for their position.
New sails, new rope. Cannons with not a
smidge of powder against the lip.

Captain Lutterell: Then you have no need to be
so gun shy as you were when you last left the
doc's infirmary.

Jules: I have less to fear now than I did in
greeting the Crown's beloved Captain.

Captain Lutterell: That is a relief to my old
bones. This is the best I can wish for. Here,
stand up. (Jules stands) Yes, this is how it
should end, shouldn't it? You were a great
quartermaster for me. I want to see the
Captain. Right. Go and bring him. Before the
pantheon, the whole of Squanderer's Bay
owes this Madam the riches within all the
holds and warehouses.

Jules: Doc, mind helping me with my trunks? I should probably get myself clean for once in so many fortnights as it has been, and I have yet to have complete depth perception to navigate my locker and stocks.

Sailing Master Luther: You don't need to hurry so; it won't be for some time.

Captain Lutterell: Go, Doc. Help them out. We'll bid Jules good luck with their new venture tomorrow.

Sailing Master Luther: We don't have enough in our larders and cargo holds for a feast for both crews.

Captain Lutterell: You needn't worry, Luther. I've left word with Cook to hire hands to help with preparations. (Exit Sailing Master Luther) And that leaves only me to this deck. I guess, in the end, I am the one handing over this contract. I should speak with Parker. It is a relief, I must say, to see them well cared for. A privateer life was never where they should have laid their anchor.

Exit Captain Lutterell

SCENE 3

NORTH DOCKS: JULES'S CABIN ON *The Black Albatross*

Enter Jules, packing bags, followed by Sailing Master Luther

Jules: He's my husband! You think I'm just going to forgo my vows to be plucked up by that ignoramus pig-headed lout looking for another feather in his cap?

Sailing Master Luther: Repeat this for me again. You got married? To a Blade? By a brothel captain?

Jules: Yeah. I did. Husband and my quartermaster.

Sailing Master Luther: What do you mean 'your quartermaster'? He's no quartermaster. The Blade dissolved, just like us Albatrosses.

Jules: He is my quartermaster. We've taken holding of The Red Lantern. I'm the captain now, Luther. Or, at least, as long as no one goes and throws a fit, I will be at the end of the week once the paperwork has gone through a great many official fingers and

stamps. You think I would give up love, or a
ship, just to join the Navy for the Crown? You
don't know me very well, do you? I've
wanted out from under Lutterell's thumb for
years and now I get the opportunity to
become something more than just another
navigator.

No, man. No.

That longing to see the sun blossom on the
horizon is the same feeling I get when
Roman walks by. And you know what? I'm
keeping that feeling.

If you think me mad, check with the Privateer's
Office. We're registered. Lutterell just had to
look at that massive pile of papers on his
desk to see my resignation letter. Did he?
No? That's not my fault or my problem. See
to it that Parker lays off. I have no business
with that man.

Exit Jules and Sailing Master Luther

SCENE 4

ACT 4, SCENE 4

NORTH DOCKS:
HALL IN
The Black Albatross

Enter Sailing Master Luther and Doc

> **Sailing Master Luther:** Cook is asking for spices and wanted to know if you had any hidden in that apothecary chest of yours.
>
> **Doc:** I can go rummage around and see what's left. I might have something.

Enter Captain Lutterell

> **Captain Lutterell:** It is already well past the hour to be up and awake. Go into the market and find the spices there. No need to delve into your own warehouse, Doc.
>
> **Doc:** Off with you, Captain. You were told to go rest. Your heart is not what it was ten years ago, you old sea turtle. Why are you here getting involved in Cook's affairs?
>
> **Captain Lutterell:** It's still plenty strong enough to see me through a few rumpled sheets in a berth or two.

Sailing Master Luther: You might be strong enough to get it up; doesn't mean you won't die one of these days and haunt the poor lily who holds your lifeless form. Have some thought for others.

Exit Sailing Master Luther and Doc

Captain Lutterell: Ah, he's just jealous, just jealous is all. Maybe he should go talk to Madam Linley about a berth.

Enter Galley Help with produce and cargo

What's for dinner tonight?
First Galley Help: Ingredients for Cook. He hasn't told me what he's doing.
Captain Lutterell: Be off with you then if you cannot satisfy my curiosity.

Exit the First Galley Help

You'll need kindling split better than this. Call on Palmer; he knows where to find the stack.
Second Galley Help: Sir, I needn't bother Palmer, who already has been strung in every which way to see to the warehouse being unloaded and the ship's insides gutted in time to be sold to be managing a feast to say goodbye to Jules.
Captain Lutterell: Right. Right. He is already busy. We are already strung thin. The day is already half past, and the feast approaches. I

must see to Captain Parker; he's coming
with the band. At least, he said he'd bring his
sailors who could lay hand to a string and a
pipe without insult. Oh, here he comes now.

(Music plays offstage)

Doc, Sailing Master, Doc I say!

Enter Doc

Go fetch Jules. Get them ready. Captain Parker
has come to collect his quartermaster, and
there will be a feast to bid them farewell. To
bid the crew farewell, really. It is a pity to say
goodbye after so many years. I must go talk
with Captain Parker. Hurry.

Exeunt all

SCENE 5

NORTH DOCKS: JULES'S CABIN
ON
The Black Albatross

Enter Doc

Doc: Jules! Jules! No. Where'd you go? Oh, this isn't going to be good. You should have told me. No, you flighty pigeon. You wouldn't have.

Enter Sailing Master Luther

Sailing Master Luther: What are you going on about, man?

Doc: What do we do?

Sailing Master Luther: Where are they?

Doc: I don't know. I don't. I grabbed some things they left in the infirmary and came back, and they were gone. Did they come past you?

Sailing Master: No. And they would have either had to come through me or you to have left this hall.

Enter Captain Lutterell

> **Captain Lutterell:** What seems to be the matter?
>
> **Doc:** Jules is gone.
>
> **Sailing Master Luther:** There's no note. They just disappeared, like a ghost through a wall.
>
> **Captain Lutterell:** Find them. Now! Captain Parker is here and keen to take his quartermaster. I'd rather he not take after us as pirates and put us to the gallows' rope for failing to hand Jules over.
>
> **Doc:** He wouldn't!
>
> **Sailing Master Luther:** Have you seen this guy?
>
> **Captain Lutterell:** He would. And we would all force a dancer's jealousy by how merrily our toes would jump upon the gallows' decking.

Enter Madam Linley and Captain Parker with entourage

> **Madam Linley:** Come now, where is the quartermaster?
>
> **Captain Lutterell:** They are already ahead of us.
>
> (to Captain Parker) Oh, Captain. How nice to see you wanting to greet your quartermaster so early on in the day. We will have everything ready shortly.
>
> **Captain Parker:** Where is Jules?
>
> **Sailing Master Luther:** Out catching some fresh air for the moment.
>
> **Doc:** Admiring the view from The Black Alba-

tross's deck one last time before finding their footing on another.

Captain Parker: I will join them.

Captain Lutterell: Let them have a moment. They spent most of their adolescence and adulthood amongst these masts and cabins. Let them have their last goodbye. It would be like saying farewell to a mother's arms; you would not have the heart to rip that moment away from any child, would you?

Madam Linley: I don't believe the fair Captain Parker would be so cruel as to do something so unspeakable, Captain Lutterell.

Captain Lutterell: No, this is Captain Parker we're speaking of, aye? A man known to listen to all sides before laying down judgement. He isn't liable to trickery or impatience.

Madam Linley: They should come back soon. As it is, I can search them out later. One should find peace with the house that raised them and go from their mother's skirts to seek out their own stretch of sky. I would not get in the way of that first step to satisfy my own desires. To let go and watch them wander and find their own path. It is a beautiful thing, watching children grow into themselves, loosening their ropes, and dropping their sail to catch the wind. To steer into it and ride the wave that takes them into the world. It is a time of wrenching heartache and desire. It would do none of us any good to waylay their last look upon their home.

With that, I will say my goodbyes then and
encourage you to return to your men who
await a feast.

*Exeunt Madam Linley, Captain Lutterell, Sailing Master Luther,
and Captain Parker*

Lieutenant: Then, I guess I'm not needed here
at the moment?

Doc: No, not so much right now. Go, join the rest
of the crew. There's nothing to see here save
a berth that will no longer house its
favourite resident.

Exit Doc

Lieutenant: To think of a last parting. Aye, I
missed my home for some time when the sea
took me away from my mother's shores. It
would be no easy task to put on a mask of
happiness now.

Palmer: Lieutenant, a lute lies at your hip. If you
play, would you play to ease my heart?

Lieutenant: Why to ease your heart?

Palmer: For it is not just Jules's leaving us that
has us in a woeful way. We all must leave
upon our separate paths. This is a breaking
of an entire family, many families, sir, and it
is a painful day to go through the quiet
motions of life with no string to bring forth a
gentle tune to turn the mind from it.

Lieutenant: You act as if you are dying.

Palmer: If I did not act, I would surely die.

Lieutenant: I will not play for you here.

Palmer: You are a banker, not a Lieutenant.

Lieutenant: And you are a romantic, not a cabin boy.

Palmer: Never so much as the person who once kept this berth. You were brought along to play for the feast. Play for me, will you not?

Lieutenant: The feast it will be, and no other time. I would not raise the captain's ire more than a shrimp would tempt a tuna.

Sailor: Don't speak so loud. These walls are thin, and he'll know it is you who speak of him as such.

Palmer: I thought your captain was a fair man.

Lieutenant: Fair in so far as the bleach that cleans the blood from his uniform at night.

Palmer: Does he go through the bottle?

Ensign: He buys in bulk.

Palmer: And he would have our quartermaster.

Ensign: He will have anyone he so pleases.

Palmer: I wish for my friend to never take up with this man then.

Lieutenant: I would not wish to be aboard the ship if your friend does not make their presence known soon.

Midshipman: I'd rather swim with sharks.

Exeunt all

ACT 5

SCENE 1

ACT 5, SCENE 1

ATOLL OF THE GIANTS: HALF-MOON BAY MARKET.

Enter Roman and Babe, going to Jeweller's shop

Roman: To live within a dream, or within reality? I know not where I find my footing now. We will be up and away, upon Poseidon's swell to a paradise. To find a ghost. To answer the riddle of the lighthouse. It is a dream. Or a tale. One time immemorial forgot. To have found a hand to rest mine in, one to live for and die with. Is that not a morose thought? A nightmare? To have found love and yet know of mortality. I find myself invincible yet vulnerable. Is that what it is to share the weight of one's heart? I would not wish it on my worst enemy, and yet I would claim it to the world that it is mine. Love has found me, and I will keep it clasped close, for I fear, like a dove pulled from its cage, it will fly away and disappear.

Enter Roman's servant Babe

Do you come with news of the Bay? What do you know, Babe? Have you brought word from the madam? Of my spouse? Is my aunt in good health? Is Jules well? That question being the most pressing. Nothing will be amiss if they are fine.

Babe: Then they are fine, and nothing is amiss. They have pulled their lines to run from Parker's persistence, and they face the waves of their first voyage to the ships' graveyard. I saw the lines cut and came to tell you of the meeting place. Forgive me. That may not be the news you were looking for, sir.

Roman: The Red Lantern lights its way already? The stars would not see me venture with my love on their first voyage as captain—and to a graveyard, no less. Fetch me my writing materials. I must send a letter to have the Jeweller ready.

Babe: Sir, patience. If you rush this transaction, there will be less money there for the voyage than if you take Chronos at his word and bide time until Achlys's fog settles amongst the ribs of the ships tonight.

Roman: Did Madam or Jules leave word with you on where I was to find them in the graveyard?

Babe: No, good sir. Parker was pressing his advantage to gain on the ship-of-the-line's decking, and neither Jules nor Madam were slowing for his brigantine. Madam's forty guns lay ready for his approach. She would have laid waste if he'd presented a broadside. There was no time to leave a letter with me.

Roman: I would not leave my beloved to face a battle at sea. Alright. Get yourself to the Jeweller's and have him ready for me. I will gather the last of the supplies, and we will make our way.

Exit Babe

I have only just taken your hand, my dear Jules. I will not lose you now, my love. Neither cannon nor rapier shall steal my dearest treasure from me. If ever there were a need to press blade to heart, now is the time. The sea will sparkle like so many rubies laid out in the sun.

Roman enters the Jeweller's shop, where the Jeweller waits

Jeweller: I don't peddle in pearls. Too many here with the monster oysters in the area. If you think you'll get a fair price from me for bivalve spitballs, look elsewhere.

Roman: Pearls are second-rate at best, my fine fellow. No. I wouldn't think to lay upon you a pearl necklace or ring that I would not my own dearest. Hear me, good Jeweller, and see what it is I would trade for a sum of fair coinage.

Jeweller: If it is not pearl, and it is of a quality, then I will spare you fair coin.

Roman: What are your thoughts on a blue

diamond inlaid into a jadeite pendant? One obtained in Couer from a lovely noble on hard luck?

Jeweller: You have documents proving the transaction? I do not deal in stolen goods.

Roman: Never fear; here is the script, made out to a Mx. Road. And here is my contract with The Red Lantern proving my identity as Roman Verne-Road.

Jeweller: It is the finest piece I have seen. I would not be able to give you a fair price, but I will help you put it on auction for a cut of the placement fee.

Roman: I will leave it in your hands.

Exit Roman and Jeweller

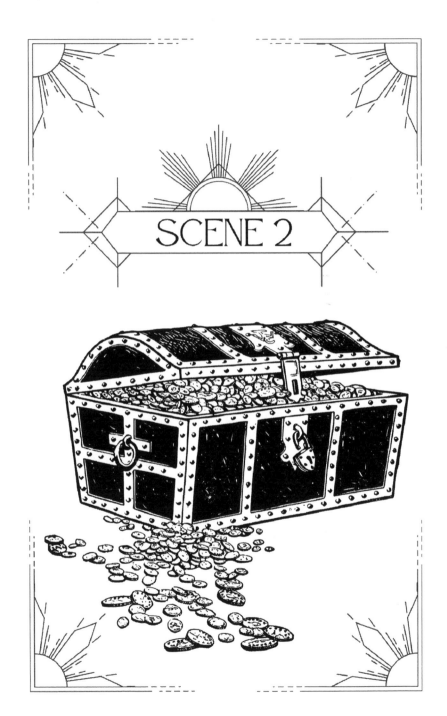

SCENE 2

ACT 5, SCENE 2

Enter Madam Josephina and Madam Linley

Madam Josephina: So, little Rome finally found himself a Caesar worth going to war for?

Madam Linley: And his Caesar came with a rather fine dowry.

Madam Josephina: Caesar is paying for this campaign and not the citizens?

Madam Linley: To the benefit of all under the Roman empire, Caesar is sharing all his holdings. A set of new maps along with provisions for a half year of voyage. Jules even registered for trade rights along the map lines with the Privateer's Office.

Madam Josephina: That's what has Roman off in Half-Moon?

Madam Linley: Jules said Roman's going to exchange the treasure from a haul they made in Couer for a cheque that'll pay for us to live in relative ease and for them to sail until they reach the edge of the world, if not farther.

Madam Josephina: Honestly, it will be nice to hear him back to floral language. I'm not sure I like it when he's talking seriously; when he steps into reality and the world is no longer tinged with roses. His reality. It's ice on the sails when you desperately want to be in port and yet you're forty leagues away with the wind pushing against you. He and Jules are stressed, but for the number of nights they both have spent in our company, this is the first time I can really say they seem happy. What do you think of that, Linley? Love can be found in happiness?

Madam Linley: Who knew it would take only one Road to lead Roman into love? A Verne of all people finding it? I would not wish to be pirate or sailor to come between him and his captain.

Exeunt Madam Linley and Madam Josephina

SCENE 3

FIDDLER'S GREEN: A SHIPS' GRAVEYARD

Enter Captain Parker with Gunner

Captain Parker: I either need a light or none at all in this gloom. The ever-present deviation of the flame is doing nothing for my sights. Where are they? Damn. I was to have the best quartermaster this side of the Whirlpool. To traverse the graveyard ships to find one measly little—

Gunner puts out the torch

Gunner: This place gives me the creeps, Admiral.

Gunner moves away

Captain Parker: Not an admiral yet, you piss-faced feck. I would be if that half-blind jackass had known what was best for them and just signed my contract. They can't do this to me! Bull. There's no way they'd have the guts to ditch a contract with the Albatross to go off on their own with some Blade. Everyone knows those crews don't get along. (Gunner whistles) Husband? Jules called him a husband? He'll lead me right to their ship. Then I'll make them see this foolhardy journey is just a passing phase of rebellion. They'll come back and sign back into the fleet.

Captain Parker hides
Enter Roman and Babe

Roman: They're good. I knew they could navigate just as good, if not better, but to hide the ship in this nest of detritus? Here, help me over this. A bright red ship can't just get lost in here, yet lost it is. If only I hadn't gotten myself turned around and ended up on the wrong dock. Their plan of a second rendezvous point is my one saving grace.

Babe: Are you sure you want me to join your crew, sir? Honestly?

Roman: I would be at a loss if I didn't have you as part of our crew, Babe. Malone will be disappointed too if you don't come with us. However, I leave it to you if you truly wish to ship out with us. The seas are a different beast than what you've experienced so far.

Babe: Then allow me to help you search for the ship. Do you know if it was floating loaded? That'll rule out some of these low-mounded

ships if it's light in the water. This place goes
on forever.

Babe wanders off in search of The Red Lantern

Roman: (speaking to Fiddler's Green) I don't
want any of these ghost ships. Give me the
living ship nestled in your decaying chest
like a beating heart. I have business with the
one who makes it pulse, and I waste time
dallying through your rotting ribs.

Roman scurries across planks and hulls

Captain Parker: (speaking to himself) Damn
the man! The one who led the Albatross
quartermaster astray with sweet words and
hollow promises. To have taken not only one
quartermaster from a captain, but to take off
with the Blade's boatswain while he was
injured? To disappear with the Albatross's
doctor and a page boy? What is he playing
at? A revolution? His Majesty will not be
pleased to learn of two of his privateers
fighting amongst themselves, and less so to
know it has factioned off into a third. (to
Roman) In the name of His Majesty, you will
not step one more foot from your position. I
am taking you in for mutiny. By dissolving
your contract without permission from your
overseeing officer, you have committed a
felony against the Crown.

Roman: Go eat mud, Parker. You're just pissed
off that you didn't get Jules for your crew,
and now you're making up shit that doesn't

exist in the legal codes, and both of us know it. Within the Navy, yes. Within the privateer code, I can dissolve my contract within reason as long as I provide in writing my valid reasoning for doing so. Name changes dissolve the contract immediately because the name isn't what is on the doc anymore. Montgomery has my letter of withdrawal, and you'd know that if you talked to both captains and not just Lutterell. Did you even ask if there was a letter of withdrawal on his desk from Jules? Or did you think I was going to be stupid enough to not know the legal workings of the privateer enterprise? I've sent my registry of ship name and flag to the Inter-Waters office of His Majesty's services as a new quartermaster under Jules. You want them as your quartermaster? They are already a captain in His Majesty's Privateers, you ill-bred son of a jackass.

Captain Parker: And yet you fled as soon as the ink was on the paper. You've done something criminal.

Roman: Do you have a search warrant with sufficient probable cause for that statement? I may be a quartermaster that enjoys a turn of phrase more than the average man. That does not mean I don't know my rights inside and out. In this type of working environment, it behoves me to know it more than you. You go crying to the Naval office, they'll clean up after you. Me? I get hanged if I step one foot in the wrong direction by accident.

You want to pursue this? (to Gunner) Go
fetch me the Governor or one of his atten-
dants. They'll know I speak the truth.
Gunner: But...I...wait...

Exit Gunner at a run

Captain Parker: You would call the Governor
here for a simple spat?
Roman: I would call the Governor here because
you threatened to arrest me on false charges
and that in and of itself is a crime prose-
cutable by the Crown. Do you want to press
this?

Exit Captain Parker at a run

Roman: What an arrogant prick. Now, back to
the task at hand. Where did my beloved hide
our ship? (Roman searches) Is it that the
ship has lost its colour in these dark waters?
Even my clothing, bright as they are, are dim
in this fog. The stars, hiding behind thick
clouds, are of no help in this. Would I recognise The Red Lantern amongst this debris as
it is all of the same shade now? Not that I can
willingly admit. I may have visited often, but
I've never paid attention to its masts. To its
rigging. To the decks and the hull. It was a
ship, like any other. But now it is my ship.
Am I a bridegroom married who never looks
upon his bride's face? Who does not recognise her in the market? Who is at risk of

falling madly in love with her and hiding the affair from her, only to be made a fool years later when she speaks? (Roman sees ship in front of him) No. I shall be no blind bridegroom. My beloved and their ship. At last I find you. Jules! Let's be off. We've a world to discover.

Enter Madam Linley and Babe on ship where a ladder is lowered
Roman climbs rope ladder

> **Madam Linley**: Jules is in the captain's quarters working out our first stop.

Exit Roman

> **Babe**: Where are we heading then, if you are no longer captain of this ship, Linley?
> **Madam Linley**: To paradise. I would wish nothing else than to give my lilies somewhere to take root, where no one picks their petals for personal pleasures. That was my price for marrying those two and filing their contracts. They got the ship. We got paradise. I want for us to flower in the sun and sleep upon a motionless bed. And what of you, Babe? What will you do now that you've joined the crew?
> **Babe**: I believe I am not yet ready for Paradise. I hear tale, though, of a Lighthouse at the end of the world. One with gold stacked to the lantern. I hope to see it with my own eyes.
> **Madam Linley:** You would travel with Jules's

crew to see this fantasy?

Babe: If Roman has found a captain worth following to the edge of the world, I will gladly tether myself to the mast and find out what monsters lay beyond these raging seas.

Madam Linley: Your trust is deep.

Babe: As deep as Bythos's abyss and as far-flung as Aphros's foam.

Madam Linley: Will this be the way of all who come to crew The Red Lantern in the lilies' stead?

Babe: What better fate would there be than to have a flame never want to burn out? It is a sign, one to give you peace, that those who come entrust themselves to a competent captain and quartermaster.

Madam Linley: I think I see why you and Roman are such good friends. The words that lay upon your tongue like honey from the hive hold the promise of spring nectar and the knowledge of the bee.

Babe: And you have drunk these honied words before if you recognise them as such.

Madam Linley: Your captain and quartermaster overflow with them more than most. I would not see either suffer the sting of a colony grown weary of their forebearer's methods. To lay witness to the collapse of the harbour at the governor's hands, I feared all who found The Red Lantern until this time would lay waste to her deckings. In a panic, I pressed Jules to move us further, if only to ease my roving dreams. And yet my dreams

did not fly. Instead, they turned to Roman, of
him lying dead upon the docks, unable to
move us from our berth in the graveyard.

Enter Jules on deck

Jules: Madam Linley, good day! The fog lays
thick about the riggings. What is this about
Roman laying on docks? No, that was not
what you said. You said he lies dead upon
the docks? What has happened to my
husband?

A noise echoes in the fog

Madam Linley: What I fear most. They have
come to take back The Red Lantern to the
harbour. I would not wish my lilies one more
night in a garden not their own. Who would
traverse these bones to satisfy a menial lust?
Jules, let us be off and away from these piers.
We will search out a safe nest upon the
waves. Roman lies below, healthy but
searching for you.

Enter Powder Monkey One searching near the ship

Powder Monkey One: Which way?
Jules: The sun is burning off the dawn fog.
Roman does not lay in Elysium. The world
has turned the colour of cut gems, and the
horizon sparkles, beckoning. Bring it to me,
my love.

The ship leaves the graveyard
Enter Gunner and Powder Monkeys

> **Gunner:** The ground is freshly pressed about.
> Footprints not my own have turned up
> the mud.
> **Powder Monkey:** Find who has left them. We
> must have answers!
> **Powder Monkey Two:** The governor must be
> informed. The Red Lantern was not
> supposed to have left its dockings. Its ware-
> house has been unloaded. We have no
> known plan or course registered with the
> Crown. With the upheaval of the harbour,
> who knows if someone has stolen it. We
> cannot afford pirates loose in our waters.
> **Powder Monkey One:** Ahoy! Ahoy!
> **Powder Monkey Three:** They've already crested
> the pass, they'd never hear you.
> **Powder Monkey One:** Oh, yeah? What says you
> to that? (Points to The Red Lantern turning
> to stall)

Enter Governor with Market Watch

> **Governor:** What must you summon me for?
> That Parker has left my bay at the same time
> that The Red Lantern goes missing, and both
> Montgomery and Lutterell come to me
> crying of lost quartermasters. To solve the
> problems of pirates? What have I become?
> Enter Captain Lutterell and Sailing Master
> Luther

Captain Lutterell: Forgive me my claims, Governor. I wish answers as you wish for a quiet cove.

Sailing Master Luther: Why must the docks be in such disarray, Governor? What could have happened to have closed the market, seen The Red Lantern cut loose its ties, see Parker turn tail to run across the water?

Governor: You were tasked with stalling your crew, and yet blade met heart and cleaved you from the Crown.

Powder Monkey One: The Red Lantern is coming back around, Gov! They can answer these questions and set right what has happened in your town.

Governor: They have much to answer for.

Powder Monkey One: They've run up the flag, Governor. They'll only come passing about; be prepared for a short conversation.

Captain Lutterell: Aye, I see, I see. What is there to ask other than if all who serve its passage lie safe within its hull?

Sailing Master Luther: I would that Jules was found lying safe within, if only to reassure me of their life. I would not wish my days on the beach watching the waves come in, knowing that they met their end before I.

Governor: When all is said and done, Luther, I wish to see a happier sunrise than the low night we must meet here. That you have seen nothing of your quartermaster since this time yesterday does concern me for how much you talked of them being dependable.

Captain Montgomery: I have seen nothing of their passage. They have gone, like a ghost in the night. I fear revenge between an Albatross and a Blade has seen both our quartermasters to a grave within Poseidon's heart. May he guide them through the waves as they guided our mortal passage.

Governor: It is I who upheaved the docks and bid you take your leave. You and The Black Albatross both. If I had kept my head, then maybe...

Captain Montgomery: I would not have Roman's and Jules's leaving blamed upon your actions.

Governor: Then may you and Lutterell both lay down your blades and make a truce fitting of the dead.

Madam Linley: Good evening to you, Governor. If you're looking for the Captain and the Quartermaster, they are aloft to the helm and guiding us as far from these waters as the sail will take them.

Governor: Are you not Captain, Madam?

Madam Linley: Has no one ever looked at the documents? Bureaucrats. Captain Jules and Quartermaster Roman. Why must those who have done what they must do doubly so for those who have not?

Governor: I saw Parker pursue your ship from the bay with some speed and feared the worst for you and yours.

Babe: No fear. No fear at all, Gov! We are away and off on a new adventure. Captain Jules

and Quartermaster Roman have us well at
hand. Let there be no ill will left between
your bay and the crews within it. We must
catch the high tide as it rolls out if we wish
to escape the breakers. Goodbye!

Ship leaves

Governor: Captain? Quartermaster? Of The Red
Lantern? Why has no one informed us of
such? Then the ship is not in the hands of
pirates?

Gunner: Depends on your definition.

Governor: Gunner?

Captain Lutterell: Jules is captain? They're the
captain of their own ship? Not quartermas-
tered to the Crown?

Captain Montgomery: It looks like they
stepped out of our shadows and grew the
height of the mast while we weren't looking,
huh, Lutterell?

Captain Lutterell: I don't need you saying it.
But yes. It looks like my fears are misplaced,
as they always have been, Montgomery.

Governor: Does no one in this bay read a
contract? And this is why you two have been
at each other's neck for years, hasn't it?
Some petty misunderstanding? Pirates!

Exeunt all

ABOUT THE AUTHOR

Chapel Orahamm started out as a pen name for Thornton Gibson and soon turned into their Line & Substance Editing business. Still using it as a pen name for the most part, they enjoy writing fiction and producing useful logbooks for authors. They joined up with Skullgate in writing short stories for a couple anthologies and ended up falling in love with the idea of creating a pirate-based Shakespearean play on the knowledge that it used to be common practice for privateers and pirates to memorise plays seen at operas and act them out on board ship as a form of entertainment—the things people did when TV didn't exist.

Despising the tragic ending of Romeo and Juliet, they set out to explore the story with a couple good twists.

They are still debating whether taking up the rest of Shakespeare's works and turning them into a pirate themed anthology would be an interesting course to follow.

ABOUT SKULLGATE MEDIA

Skullgate Media is a member-owned publishing collective. Our goal is to publish exciting and innovative fiction across a wide range of genres with a focus on speculative fiction, weird fiction, and sci-fi fantasy. We value friendly collaboration, wild imagination, and shared worlds, with the general belief that the best way for authors to succeed is to help one another. Instead of working in isolation, the members of Skullgate media have come together to pool our experience and various skill sets in order to complete the entire publishing process in-house: from drafting and beta-reading, to layout and copy-editing, to website design and marketing.

Learn about all Skullgate's projects at skullgatemedia.com, and follow us on Twitter as @skullgatemedia to learn how you can get involved with our special brand of literary strangeness.

Made in the USA
Columbia, SC
14 July 2022

63389290R00124